Captivating the Earl

The Country House Romantic Mysteries
Book 3

by
Audrey Harrison

ARE YOU SIGNED UP FOR DRAGONBLADE'S BLOG?

You'll get the latest news and information on exclusive giveaways, exclusive excerpts, coming releases, sales, free books, cover reveals and more.

Check out our complete list of authors, too!

No spam, no junk. That's a promise!

Sign Up Here

www.dragonbladepublishing.com

Dearest Reader;

Thank you for your support of a small press. At Dragonblade Publishing, we strive to bring you the highest quality Historical Romance from some of the best authors in the business. Without your support, there is no 'us', so we sincerely hope you adore these stories and find some new favorite authors along the way.

Happy Reading!

CEO, Dragonblade Publishing

Chapter One

Hampshire 1812

"**H**ENRY, YOU HAVE indulged our baby brother to the point that you have almost been as bad as Papa was in his neglect," Ruth Parkinson said, her sympathetic smile taking away the sting her words might have caused. It was one of her regular complaints to her brother, made numerous times over the years. As he was now holding a party at the request of said brother, she was, not for the first time, pointing out the error of her younger brother's decision. "Can you imagine what you would say if I spoiled my boys half as much as you do Sidney?"

"You are speaking as if it would be a possibility." Lord Henry Gosforth was sprawled casually in his leather chair in a way that would be unacceptable if he was in polite company, and not with family. "With Edwin as a husband, you would not dare make the boys soft, as he so eloquently puts it."

"Do not mock my husband," Ruth huffed. "You know he is a very patient man."

"He has to be, with you as his wife." Henry responded as only a long-suffering sibling could.

"As the eldest, it is my role to speak my mind. Just because you hold the title does not mean my opinions do not count."

Henry stretched out his long legs and crossed them at the

ankle. "I always bow to your wishes. Sidney is not the only one in the family who is over-indulged." He knew full well that Ruth could not argue the point; he was benevolent to both his siblings. He resided in the grand Palladian mansion that was the Earl of Gosforth's country seat, but he was more than generous with the family wealth. They were seated in Henry's study, surrounded by furniture that was Henry's only self-indulgence, replacing everything that reminded him of his father. There were enough reminders in the rest of the three-storey house. And Henry needed one room that held no memories of the man.

Ruth gave a harumph at his words, shaking her head at her younger brother. "You always have an answer to everything." They were close, only a year separating them, her being thirty to his nine and twenty, but their shared history had made them rely on each other even more than was usual for siblings.

Henry had smiled at her words, something Ruth wished would happen more. It lightened his features, making him look more like the brother she knew he could have been had their circumstances been different. She was fully aware that he hid his feelings by keeping everyone at a distance—even their younger brother. In many respects, Henry had taken on the role of father to Sidney, instead of that of an older brother. Understanding why he wrapped himself in a protective layer did not stop her from wishing that he was not afraid to trust others. They had all been let down by the people who should have had their best interests at heart, but it seemed to have affected Henry the most.

Her tone softened. "You need to be firm with him. Too much of your time is spent getting him out of scrapes or indulging his flights of fancy when you should be enjoying the single state before it is time to settle down."

"Here was I, enjoying the fact that a full five minutes had gone by without you mentioning my marrying. It is surely a record."

"I wonder if society appreciates that beneath that aloof exterior lies a man refusing to acknowledge there is someone out there, just waiting for him. They are under the illusion that you are looking for a wife."

"That is because you keep spreading gossip to that effect." Henry laughed, his green eyes sparkling at his sister in genuine amusement. "I need to speak to Edwin about the number of novels you must be reading to come out with comments like *there is someone waiting for me*. What rubbish!"

"He would agree with me that a bit of romance would do you the world of good." She dismissed his censure with a wave of her hand. "To get back to the point of your constant overindulging of the baby of the family, this party is a perfect example. Why are you holding a ten-day gathering for him just so he can show off his latest hobby? I mean, ballooning! I am beginning to question our brother's sanity."

"I thought it would be the perfect opportunity to let him work off some of his need for constant excitement and entertainment. Maybe, after this party, he might finally accept his place in society and a career."

"And that could not be achieved without putting yourself to so much trouble?"

"He said it would help to smooth the feathers of his friends when he tells them he will no longer be a part of their schemes. His main donor, especially, will not be happy. He is hoping that a party invitation will soften the blow."

"And you swallowed that Banbury tale?" It was clear Ruth did not believe her younger brother's words and looked surprised that Henry did.

"Not really, but I thought he would not be able to disregard my demand that he choose a career if I went along with his part of the bargain."

"I would say that your thoughts are flawed, but it is too late now as you have agreed to it. I take it you would like my involvement in the planning of the party?"

"Would you mind?" Henry grimaced. "I never know who to invite to these blasted things at the best of times."

"And yet you still indulged him."

"It might reassure you to know that I have told him this is the last time I will pander to his wishes."

"I am sure I have heard that before."

"This time it is different. I have come to the conclusion that by trying to make up for our father's faults, I am actually doing Sidney more harm than good."

"At last, he sees the light! Probably ten years too late, but nevertheless it is progress." Ruth raised her hands in mock astonishment.

"I accept that I might deserve that response," Henry responded dryly. "I have told him that after the house party he browbeat me into, he has to tell me what he wishes to do with his life."

"And when he shrugs his shoulders and smiles at you, knowing full well how he has twisted you around his little finger in the past and always got his own way? What then?"

"I have already shown him the papers on my desk. If he does not make a decision, I will send them off."

"Please say he is to take orders."

"Try not to sound quite so gleeful, thinking that what I am offering him is something he would not like. It seems you have a wicked streak in you."

"I am my father's daughter. Oh, come now, I am teasing." Ruth responded to the immediate glower her words had caused.

"You are nothing like him. I wish you would not even joke about such a thing."

"One of us has to be light-hearted. But this is all taking us away from what you have planned for our spoiled little brother's future employ."

"I have told him that I will purchase a commission for him if he does not make a decision."

"That is not much of a punishment for him! He will look dashing in his uniform and be even more uncontrollable than he is now, strutting around town."

There was a mischievous glint in Henry's eyes. "I might have had the wrong forms drawn up. By accident, of course. He actually paled when he saw the forms were for the regulars and not the cavalry."

Ruth burst into laughter, clapping her hands. "Oh, how I wished I had seen his expression."

"It was priceless."

"There is hope for you yet, brother. Although knowing Sidney, he will throw himself out of the blasted hot air balloon and break his leg, just so you cannot send him to be a common soldier."

"Do not even suggest that within his hearing," Henry said. "We both know he would act on that idea if he thought it would release him from making a decision. You should just appreciate the fact that I am forcing the issue, even as I understand that at three and twenty, he should be acting more responsible."

Ruth took a moment to glance around the dark mahogany elegance of what had once been their father's study, acutely aware that the room held less than happy memories for Henry. She was glad that her brother had changed enough of it to make it his own. "Let us make this party a big one," she announced.

"Why? You were against it not many minutes ago. Can we not just make it small and get it out of the way?"

"It could be the last time the three of us are together for a while if Sidney is to start his career. We need to make the most of this time. We do not get together as often as we should."

"Considering Sidney will be showing off his flying skills and charming a captive audience while we will be acting as hosts, I cannot see many private tête-à-têtes going on between us."

"True, but hopefully I will be able to use the little time we are together to convince Sidney to sign up to whatever he decides to do for the longest period possible."

"Anyone would think you dislike our younger brother."

"If he did not take advantage of the head of the family so much, I would certainly like him better."

"His actions have no bearing on my decisions, either family-related or about my personal life."

"Do they not?"

Henry was beginning to feel uncomfortable at Ruth's prob-
ing; it was stirring emotions that he would much rather keep
pushed aside. He loved his sister dearly, but when she got a bee in
her bonnet about Sidney, she would bring up all the old wounds
to make him try and see sense. "He knows I am in all seriousness."

"But you never kept to your threats before now. What has
changed?"

"As I have admitted to you, I have accepted that I have been
wrong in indulging him so much. Sidney is in for a shock if he
does not heed my threat. You have my word in that regard."

"I hope you stick to your guns. It will be better for both of
you in the long term."

"There is no need to worry. I will."

"Good. Then there is no time like the present to go and speak
to Cook about what we can serve and Mrs. Repton about
preparing the rooms. I have a mind to fill them all."

"Thank you, I appreciate your help, but there is no need to
invite quite so many."

"Oh, you know if I do something, I do it to the best of my
ability."

"Is that the same as taking things too far?"

"Do you want my help or not?"

"Yes, please."

"Good. I like acting the lady of this house; it helps create
happy memories, though I know it will be a temporary position,
for I am convinced one day you will find a woman who is good
enough for you."

"But will I be good enough for her? That is the question you
should be asking."

"I have every faith in you, my dear brother. I might consider
myself to be like our father, but you most certainly are not."
Standing, then kissing him on the cheek, Ruth left the room

intent on making their gathering the best. Lord Gosforth, her darling brother Henry, needed to find himself a wife, and this was the perfect opportunity to make him shine.

Henry had stood when Ruth left. Brother and sister were alike in many ways, both green-eyed and fair-haired, tall and athletic in build. But they were very different in personality. Ruth was almost businesslike in the way she dealt with issues; if there was a problem, she would think it through and find a solution, not worry about how it had to be achieved. Henry, on the other hand, was the deep thinker, the one who always had to consider the consequences before making a decision. It was a form of protection for him and those in his care. He never wanted his actions to hurt anyone, and he refused to let history repeat itself. If it made him over-cautious and distant, he would rather that than turn out like his father. The memories and nightmares of their father's treatment towards the family made him strive to be the exact opposite. Just the thought of being even slightly like his father was enough to make him break out in a sweat of panic.

The conversation with Ruth had unsettled him, as any reference to their father and his impact on their lives always did. Henry was seen as a reasonably handsome, rich, titled man and, at nine and twenty, very desirable for those wishing for a good match. The problem for the young ladies considering aligning themselves with Henry Brook, the Earl of Gosforth, was that no one could say that they really knew him. Oh, he was polite and perfectly pleasant to speak to, certainly not one of the *ton* who gave out cutting remarks or set-downs unnecessarily. But if someone described him as aloof, it would not be too far from the image he portrayed. It was almost as if he was constantly wearing a mask. No one truly knew him, not even Ruth or Sidney, though Ruth was the one who had come close.

He looked out of the window that revealed a small section of his vast estate. Seeing the drive that led into the wooded carriage ride, he was tempted to travel down it, take on a new name, and never return to this house, its memories and its nightmares. He had tried to shelter Sidney as much as he could, but after a recent conversation with his lawyer, he knew that he had not been kind to his brother by cosseting him. It was time Sidney was given the chance to prove himself to society.

As for himself, he was fully aware that Ruth was determined to find him a wife, but how could he, in all conscience, marry someone when he would very likely turn into a tyrant like his father had. His fear of having the same character defect as his parent kept him awake at night. How could he not be like his father, when he had the same blood pumping through his veins? His father could not have always been as cruel as he was, or his mother's family would never have allowed a match. After all, his grandfather had stepped in when he had become aware of how bad his daughter's life was. It was a pity the man had not rescued all of them at the same time.

No, he could never risk turning into the beast like the one who had created him. He would maintain the distant exterior, though he bored himself to hear the bland comments he uttered during dances and introductions. He was destined to remain unmarried, and he had to accept that, whether his heart longed for company or not. His sister, brother and nephews would have to be enough, for he would not let history repeat itself. Seeing the small similarities to his father every morning when looking into his mirror was enough of a reminder for him that he could not be too careful. He was determined to be different, even if it meant that he lived out his years alone.

ISABELLE CARRINGTON WAS fat. She knew this without the sighs and tsks her modiste gave her every time she went to be fitted for a new gown. She also did not need the comments from some members of the *ton*, who at best referred to her as the plump one, and at worst, well, there were many names that were best not repeated. As for those who came out with such comments as *at least she has a good personality*, they truly thought that they were being generous with their words and giving her a compliment.

Luckily, Isabelle had friends, good friends, who sometimes tried to compensate with too many compliments. However, she did not really mind their efforts to reassure her because, without doubt, she knew they genuinely liked her for who she was and did not judge her for what she looked like. They were the ones who kept her sane in a fickle world in which money, beauty and youth were valued over anything else. That her curves were more pronounced than was the fashion, her dresses unable to hide the swell of her hips, or the roundness of her stomach—though her mother gave her credit for her breasts needing little enhancement—they were perfectly capable of creating a pleasing silhouette without the need of extra padding. These were the thoughts that filled her mind as she was prodded and poked and fitted for new gowns suitable for a house party.

"I cannot understand why Grandfather is insisting I attend," Isabelle said to her friend Sophia, who had accompanied her to the appointment. Her mother was also there, but Isabelle needed the moral support of a friend whenever undergoing something as traumatic as a dress fitting. It was not the pleasurable experience many would enjoy. It was a time of having to face the fact that she was different from what society wished her to be, that she was in some way inferior to the slim people around her. In day-to-day life, she could ignore it, but not when she was the focus of attention. Here, she could not hide away, needing to face the disparaging remarks whilst keeping a smile on her face as if it did not matter that she was dying inside.

"It is a coveted invitation," Sophia replied.

"I am glad you are joining us, but you could always go instead of me. You could pretend to be me and make people think I have changed for the better."

Sophia frowned. "You are perfect the way you are, and we both know that I could never be as quiet or unassuming as you are—until you sing, of course. Then you completely take a room by storm. I am more likely to destroy some priceless heirloom as I try to make a good impression."

"The vase that you broke in the Bellingham's house was already damaged. It would not have shattered if it had been in perfect condition. You gave it a slight knock, nothing more."

Sophia grimaced. "They insisted it was perfect. Mother was furious, and if I live until I am ninety, my pin money will not have paid for it!"

Isabelle touched Sophia on the arm. "It really was not your fault. His lordship had startled you."

Sophia scowled. "Yes, the coxcomb had, but enough of that. This blue would suit you perfectly. It would make the colour of your eyes stand out." The material was a beautiful shade of aquamarine, matching Isabelle's eyes.

"No, no, no," tsked the modiste. "Darker is better." She moved her hands down her sides, clearly indicating the darker shades would be more slimming.

"I am a single woman. I can wear lighter shades if I like them," Isabelle said in her usual quiet way. She would not normally speak up for herself, but she loved the beautiful shade.

"Ah, but as a spinster, not a debutante, you can wear darker," the modiste replied.

"You must listen to Madame Francine," Mrs. Carrington scolded Isabelle. "She knows exactly what to do to bring out the best in you, and you know how difficult a task that is."

Isabelle was so used to hiding, avoiding attracting attention in any form, that her automatic response was to let her shoulders slump and watch with longing as Sophia relinquished the bolt of material to one of the assistants. It was exquisite, a colour and texture she had never seen before.

The moment Sophia's hands no longer held the material, Isabelle felt a surge of something inside. She wanted a beautiful dress, whether the shade was too light for her or not. And she never got to choose what she wore, but was always told by her mother or the modiste, who would try to do the impossible to make her look slimmer.

She had always put up with it without complaint; after all, she saw herself in the looking glass every day. But she was going to a party where she knew no one and for once, she wanted to feel that she had some say in how she looked.

Surprising everyone, but none more than herself, she shouted "No!" at the startled assistant as she put the bolt of material onto a pile of rejected shades and patterns.

"Isabelle!" Mrs. Carrington exclaimed. "Manners!"

"Sorry, Mother, but I want a dress in that material. If Madame Francine does not wish to make it, we could buy the fabric. I am sure I could find someone else who would be willing to make a dress for me." She could have laughed at the opposing expressions her words caused; Sophia looked delighted, while Madame Francine looked furious. The modiste's displeasure was brought home further when a few moments later a supposedly accidental misplacement of a pin made Isabelle yelp.

Unfortunately for Madame Francine, Isabelle continued to quietly insist on wishing to use the lighter material, and rather than lose out on a commission, the modiste muttered about women who were old enough and ugly enough to know better.

By the end of the session, Isabelle felt battered both emotionally and physically and was relieved when Sophia offered to buy ices for them both if they walked back. Having left Mrs. Carrington with her warnings of not walking too fast to avoid the unattractive rosy cheeks caused by exertion, Isabelle and Sophia were able to escape.

"I think it is time I learned how to make my own dresses," Isabelle said once the busy streets of London's best shopping area had swallowed them up. "If Grandfather is determined to continue paying for a fashionable wardrobe, I need a way to avoid Madame Francine."

"I am not surprised you wish to dispense with her services. What she hinted at was bad enough, but when she started venting her thoughts, it was truly awful. I am surprised your mother did not scold her."

"My mother agrees with her. To be honest, Madame Francine is not as bad as some I have visited," Isabelle confessed. "Mother insists she is the best because she does not overcharge for the extra material or work that goes into a gown. I have to accept that making dresses for me is more difficult than for others."

"I do wish you would not speak in such a way," Sophia said. "You are one of the loveliest people I know, and it is ridiculous for them to make you feel as if you are not the same as the rest of us."

Isabelle smiled a little but turned her head away from her friend.

Not caring that she stopped in the middle of a busy thoroughfare, Sophia swung in front of Isabelle. "Do not dismiss my words! You know I would not say them if I did not mean them."

"I know you are a good friend, but look at me, Sophia. I see myself every day, and even I do not like what I see. How can I expect anyone else to like this." She waved at her curves. "I am five and twenty, this is my shape, and no matter how I have starved myself, been bled, only drank whatever concoction my mother has discovered, it does not change. I have to accept my shape, but my friends need to be honest too."

"You clearly do not see what we do," Sophia said gently.

"No, you are biased because of our friendship," Isabelle said, taking off her glasses and wiping the bridge of her nose with a handkerchief. She had no need of a looking glass to know that her face would be beetroot red already because of the exercise, never mind blotchy because of tears. How did women cry prettily? She had never worked out a way to do so. "I am truly grateful, but when I hear one of you saying that I am petite, it makes my skin prickle waiting for someone to laugh at the comment."

"But you are smaller than the rest of us!"

"In height, maybe, not in girth."

"I am sorry. I did not presume what I would consider an innocent remark would cause you distress. I will be sure not to mention it again, and neither will the others, but that does not alter the fact that I wish you would believe the nice things said about you rather than listening only to the nasty comments spoken by people who are clearly not very pleasant."

"As my mother says, at least I can sing, or there would be nothing to celebrate about me at all."

"There are things I could say in response to that, but good manners and not wishing to openly disparage your mother forbid me," Sophia ground out.

Isabelle smiled, knowing her friend wished to curse her mother to the devil. "I think Grandfather considers my breaks from Mother as a reprieve from her censure, but strangers can be even worse."

"I doubt that," Sophia muttered, half to herself. "At least with this house party, you will have that beautiful gown to show yourself off in."

"I am thankful you can come with me. It will be good to have your company, especially with Cousin Eliza joining us. She can be as bad as Mother in her own way, but Grandfather is supporting us both, and she really wants to find a husband."

"She is thirty," Sophia said gently.

"I know, but perhaps she will find someone who can tolerate her ways. Listen to me! That is a horrible thing for me to say when I, too, am hurt by the comments made towards myself. I despair of my character, I really do."

"You are being honest, though. Eliza is overwhelming some-times and a little…forthright in her opinions."

"She means well."

"I know, and I am glad to be joining you both. I am surprised your mother is not insisting on joining us. It is an invitation that is desired by those not lucky enough to receive one. Lord Gosforth does not usually hold house parties."

"She says she would rather not witness my attempts to hide

when I should be doing all that I can to find myself any man who might accept me whilst Grandfather is still around to indulge me. She keeps warning me that he will not be around forever."

"Oh dear."

"Do not worry, it is her way of covering up the fact that Grandfather has insisted she should not visit him. Not if she wants to continue to receive a healthy allowance. He says he is happy to pay to keep her away and cannot believe his darling son could have been attracted to such a termagant. It does make her very angry, but I am just relieved that there is a reprieve for me with Grandfather." Isabelle smiled at the memory of the conversation between her formidable grandfather and mother.

"She should not abuse you just because you are the light of your grandfather's eye."

"I am used to her words and accusations."

Sophia changed the subject. "Do you think they will offer rides in the hot air balloon? I have seen one in Vauxhall Gardens and I longed to be onboard. It looked amazing to be above the trees, looking down on the buildings."

Isabelle laughed. "I expect to see you having wrangled a trip onboard, for if there was ever someone up for adventure, it is you."

"I hope we both find adventure."

"I am not so sure I am the adventurous type. I much prefer the quiet life. Patricia and Amelia have had so many adventures, I can live vicariously through them," she said of two of their friends.

"They found love as well as adventure."

"I would be happy with a peaceful ten days away," Isabelle said, looking forward to not seeing her mother's disappointment every day.

"In that case, we shall make sure it is."

Unfortunately, as their friends could have told them, life rarely goes to plan.

Chapter Two

LEADING HIS GRANDDAUGHTERS, Isabelle and Eliza, and Isabelle's friend, Sophia into the grand entrance hall of Gosforth House, Mr. Carrington greeted Ruth and Edwin warmly. "It is good to see you, my dear. It has been too long."

"It has. Pops would never forgive me if he knew how I have neglected you. I am fully aware that I should visit more," Ruth replied of her own grandfather, who had been great friends with Mr. Carrington.

"I miss him every day. Friends like that only come along once in a lifetime, and Alex was one of the best people I have ever known," Mr. Carrington said. "But you have your hands full running around after your brood, so I do not expect you to be visiting me, and your letters delight me. I really appreciate them. How many terrors have you now?"

"Three," Ruth said with a smile. "Not including Edwin." Chuckling at Edwin's long-suffering sigh, Mr. Carrington introduced Eliza, Isabelle and Sophia. "I hope you enjoy your time here. I hear you might be persuaded to sing for us during one of the evenings, Miss Carrington."

Isabelle glared at her grandfather. "I am sure there are many who are far more talented than I."

"Do not believe her, Mrs. Parkinson. She has the voice of an angel," Sophia said.

"It seems you have been found out, Miss Carrington," Ruth said with a grin. "Do not worry, you are surrounded by friends here. We are inclined to be pleased, which I sometimes think is half the battle when being forced to perform."

Ruth's words were said with such friendliness that Isabelle could not help but smile at her. "It is indeed."

"Then it is settled," Ruth said. "I will look forward to you being the star of the gathering."

"I have just been bamboozled into acquiescing," Isabelle laughed. "But it was so expertly done, I cannot say that I was forced into it. Very well done, Mrs. Parkinson."

"You will get used to it over the coming days," Edwin spoke for the first time, apart from the exchange of pleasantries. "She bullies everyone around her and always with a smile on her face."

Ruth rolled her eyes at her husband. "I have no idea what you mean."

"I would sing badly, Miss Carrington," Edwin said teasingly. "It is the only way to escape further requests."

"That is useful to know, for if you all think my performance is very poor, I can always blame it on being told to act in such a way by yourself."

"Happy to be of service," Edwin said with a smile. He seemed quieter than his wife, glad to let his more gregarious spouse take the lead, but his looks held nothing but affection towards her.

"You make me out to be an ogre!" Ruth said.

"No, that is my role in the family," Henry said, approaching the group. "Forgive me for not welcoming you sooner. My brother needed some advice which he thought was desperately urgent."

"And it was not?" Ruth asked.

"Of course not. When has it ever been?" Henry said and was introduced to everyone before handing them over to the housekeeper.

The party was shown to their rooms as other guests arrived. The house was large, and from the number of carriages making their way down the drive, the rooms were going to be full. Isabelle, Eliza and Sophia were to share a room, whilst Mr. Carrington was next door in one of the smaller chambers. The upper floors spread out in two directions, forming large wings; there were at least twenty bedrooms and more on the floor above.

"There must be some serious wealth in this family," Sophia said, once they were left alone in their chamber. The room was large and elegantly furnished, though not overly ornate.

"Are you going to set your cap for one of the brothers?" Isabelle teased.

"Definitely not! I have had my fill of lords and their disdain. Lord Bellingham has put me off anyone titled for a lifetime," she said of her lifelong friend, who had recently turned into her nemesis. She was even more self-conscious about her clumsiness when around him lately. "I think I should set my mind to marrying a farmer; it would be a simple life at least."

"It is important to set one's cap at the highest person one can," Eliza said, clearly missing the fact the friends were funning. "A farmer might sound well and good to you now, but never underestimate the hardship a lack of funds and hard work can bring."

Isabelle laughed. "I would not worry, Eliza. Sophia runs from the room screaming if she sees a spider; I cannot envisage her tramping through the countryside and tending animals."

"I will have to make sure he is a gentleman farmer who just needs me to remain indoors and be witty and entertaining to his fellow country folk," Sophia responded airily.

"Ah, you are teasing. I see how it is," Eliza said. "I, on the other hand, need to be serious in my assessment of every guest and look at whether or not they would be acceptable to me. For I can only commit to someone who fits my list of requirements. I refuse to accept anything less."

Isabelle and Sophia looked at Eliza, struggling with what to say. She was a tall woman, one whose build could be described as gangly with a pinched expression, hair that had become streaked with silver at an early age, strong opinions that she gave freely to anyone—whether stranger or friend—and a misplaced sense of importance. It was a sad fact that in society's eyes, she had very little to recommend her, especially with regards to a dowry. And at thirty years of age, she was no longer considered anything but a spinster.

"I think we should concentrate on enjoying the party and forget everything else." Isabelle finally broke the silence, not wishing to point out that they had been invited purely because of their connection to their grandfather and his friendship with Ruth, not that they were considered good houseguests in their own right. Two women aged five and twenty, as she and Sophia were, plus Eliza at thirty, were not invited to parties to tempt the gentlemen in attendance.

"You can do as you wish, but I am your chaperone in name only. I have told Grandfather in no uncertain terms that I refuse to waste my time trying to seek out a husband for you when I am older and need to marry first. I think it unfair that he should suggest I become your chaperone when it is obvious there is every chance I might find a husband first. I have just not had your advantages," Eliza grumbled.

"There is no need to worry about me," Isabelle said. "I am not looking to marry at all and am quite happy to spend time with Sophia."

"Then why agree to come? I would not be here unless I thought there would be opportunities for me to secure my future." Eliza was clearly astounded by Isabelle's attitude.

"For an enjoyable break? To see a part of the country I have never seen before?" Isabelle said. "One does not always have to be looking for a husband."

"At my age there is."

"As we are within five years of each other, that is hardly a great difference. I have already accepted that I will not marry, and I am content in the knowledge that I do not need to twist myself in knots trying to chase the impossible."

"Cousin, dear, your words sadden me when it is so easily fixable if you only try a little harder. If you lost some weight, it would make all the difference, for you do have a pretty face underneath all the excess," Eliza said.

"Thank you," Isabelle said with resignation; her weight was never far from Eliza's thoughts.

"You are welcome. I only have your best interests at heart, and if cousins cannot be honest with each other, it is a poor show. I advise you to eat very little while you are here so that you can show any potential suitors that you are trying to change at least. That should help your situation. Aunt May is always repining your large appetite."

Sophia looked thunderous, but Isabelle shook her head at her friend. "Thank you for your advice. I think I will go and explore the gardens," Isabelle said, leaving the room before anyone could offer to accompany her.

Needing time to be alone was all too familiar to Isabelle. People thought they had the right to judge, presume, and offer solutions; it was exhausting. Walking down the stairs and quickly through the hall, she left the house, veering into what she had seen was the start of the formal gardens.

Finding a secluded stone seat which overlooked the vista, encompassing the farmland surrounding the house, she forced her shoulders to relax. It took a while, but at last the tension started to ease, and feeling she could at last breathe, she closed her eyes and took deep, slow breaths. It did not matter what others thought. She knew this was the way she was, and although far from perfect, she had more or less accepted her shape. That she very often felt the need to hide away was the result of the actions of others, not her own desire. It was a pity they could not keep their thoughts and feelings contained the way she had to.

Hearing a noise to her left, she turned to see a farm cart entering the field in front of her. Leaning forward, she watched with interest as the first parts of the hot air balloon started to be unloaded.

"I will be watching you closely. I do not expect anything but attentiveness towards me on your part. I know how you can be when in company." A gruff voice came from behind Isabelle.

Swinging around, she could not see who had spoken because of the hedge, nor who was replying. Feeling a little awkward at eavesdropping, she tried to huddle further into the seat, hoping the pair did not venture in her direction.

"I promise I will always be by your side. You are the only person who matters to me," a soft voice answered.

"And yet I often catch you tittering at some comment or other another man has made."

"It is politeness which forces me to respond, nothing more."

There was the sound of a slap and a yelp of pain. "Do not lie to me! I see the way you look in their direction, wishing to catch their eye."

"I do not, I promise you." Another slap followed the words, and sobs filled the space.

Isabelle jumped from her seat, unable to remain hidden. She hated cruelty of any kind, probably more sensitive to it because of her own experiences, and though she usually avoided confrontation, she could not ignore someone being attacked.

Moving around the hedge that had obscured her, she was met with the sight of a barrel of a man and a much younger woman. He was puce with anger, seeming to tower over the woman, though they were not too dissimilar in height. The poor woman was sobbing, holding onto her bruised cheek.

"What the devil do you think you are doing to her? You are a beast for striking her, and I will not allow it to continue!" Isabelle said, acting completely out of character. Her own cheeks flushed when she saw Henry come around the opposite hedge in perfect time to hear her outburst, though he had not seen Mr. Daniels's actions.

"This has nothing to do with you!"

"Preventing another from being hurt for no good reason has

everything to do with anyone with a conscience."

"She is my wife, and I will treat her as I see fit! I do not need any interference from someone like you."

"A decent human being? No, I expect you do not, you damned bully, but you have it anyway. Would you like to accompany me back to the house?" Isabelle asked the woman, stepping closer, fully aware she was putting herself within striking distance of the man. "I could put something cool on your cheek."

"My lord, are you going to stand there and let this...this specimen come between myself and my wife?" the man demanded of Henry, who he had just seemed to notice.

"I am certainly not going to interfere when a genteel young woman comes to the rescue of another. Nor will I allow you to insult one of my guests or stand by while you abuse your own wife," Henry said. "You might have been invited because you help to fund Sidney's exploits, but I will not tolerate such actions within my household, Mr. Daniels."

Mr. Daniels snorted in Isabelle's general direction before stomping away, dragging his still sobbing wife along with him.

Isabelle watched them go, knowing there was nothing she could do to help Mrs. Daniels but wishing she could. "I hope I have not made things worse for her," she said mainly to herself.

"I doubt there could be little worse than being married to a man like him, Miss Carrington." Henry had been struck by the angry, cursing young woman when she had come into view. She had seemed like a timid little thing when the introductions had been carried out, but there was nothing hesitant about the way she had stood up to Daniels. Her wide blue eyes had sparked with fury, and she had seemed to grow in stature. There had been none of the meek wallflower in her manner, and it had been impressive to watch.

"You are quite right."

Henry's lips twitched despite the seriousness of what they had witnessed. "If only my brother and sister were so easy to persuade that what I say has value."

"I expect all brothers and sisters are the same."

"Probably. I am no longer surprised that you can stand in front of a roomful of people and sing after your fierce display towards Mr. Daniels."

Not knowing whether a fierce display was a good or bad thing, Isabelle flushed. "I could not stand by whilst I could hear Mrs. Daniels being struck, though I was afraid he would consider that I was an equally easy target."

"I would not have responded well to him striking out at you." Henry surprised himself by the force of his words, but he excused it by the fact he had a strong innate need to protect those under his care, and she was under his roof. Even the thought of her being attacked by Mr. Daniels made him angrier than he had ever felt and had him taking a slow breath to calm himself down. Her look of surprise at his overly forceful tone made him acknowledge that he should have been more careful with his words, or at least the way he had uttered them, and he quickly changed the subject. "Do you enjoy performing?"

"I hate it."

Henry was taken aback by her response for the second time. "Why? Do you find that cursing slips out if you forget the words?"

Isabelle laughed, though she flushed. "I can assure you that I do not normally curse, unless under extreme provocation."

"That is good to know, but if that is the case then why do you hate being asked to perform? I doubt your grandfather would promote you if you had no talent. And do not all young women enjoy showing off their skills?"

Henry's words caused a laugh. "Many families promote the ones they feel have talent, but I would much rather sit and watch. I admit that I am able to hold a tune, though that sounds very conceited."

"Then why the reluctance?" Henry never usually took the trouble to spend so much time with a guest; heck, he hardly ever invited anyone to the estate now that Ruth was married. They were quite far from the house and unchaperoned, but he was intrigued by the way she had stood up to Daniels, yet she seemed the epitome of the term wallflower.

"If you were me, would you?" Isabelle asked. When Henry did not answer immediately, she shrugged. "I thought not. I am sorry for cursing a guest. I can assure you that I do not make a habit of it. Good day, my lord." Isabelle stepped around Henry and hurried back to the house.

Henry sighed. This was exactly why he did not interact with young women. Though she was not a debutante, she had probably expected him to flatter her into thinking that he was desperate to hear her. He was not the type of man for uttering meaningless words or raising hopes in an unmarried woman, though she was certainly out of the ordinary in some respects. She filled her dress in a way that promised luscious curves underneath and had the most beautiful eyes he had ever seen, set in an expressive face. Blast it, he could not allow himself to be attracted to a guest, no matter that he thought her delightful. He had to admire her spirit, too, but having one appealing guest did not make him any more comfortable with the house party, especially with the likes of Daniels being invited, though he was the ballooning group's chief sponsor.

He had given in to Sidney, and though he knew Ruth was correct, he should have stopped indulging Sidney years ago, but she did not know what he had been told in no uncertain terms by their father or discovered when he inherited the title. In his own way, he was trying to make up for the wrongs of the past, though he was coming to the conclusion that no matter what he did, there would be consequences to face at some point in the future. It was a painful ache inside him that he had done everything he could to protect Sidney, but it most likely would be for naught. There could be those in society who knew far more about what had gone on around the time of Sidney's birth than he did.

Terrified of letting his family down, he put himself in awkward situations, none more than having a houseful of guests. He had not thought through the speculation he would create by having a house party. People would assume it was for something other than giving in to Sidney, trying to make up for the sense of abandonment they all felt at different levels; they would presume the single lord was looking for a wife. It was only the first day of the gathering, and he already wished each of his guests far away. It was going to be a long ten days.

Chapter Three

S IDNEY BROOK, YOUNGEST of the Brook children, and the one to constantly give his older siblings a headache, bounded into Henry's study, all smiles and unbridled excitement. "We have the equipment here. It is all coming together," Sidney said, flinging himself in the chair in front of Henry's desk. "This is going to go down in history as the best house party ever."

"I can scarcely contain my excitement," Henry responded, barely looking up from scanning a pile of papers.

"You should be thanking me. When we find you a wife, you will have to accept that this was a good idea."

"Since when did you decide that I needed to marry? Has Ruth been persuading you to browbeat me into submission?"

Sidney laughed, hazel eyes twinkling. "You know full well it is time you had an heir."

"You are my heir."

Waving his hand dismissively, Sidney shook his head. "I am not made to be the head of the family. I would waste the fortune and let the house go to rack and ruin."

His brother's final words caused Henry to smile. "You probably would, you coxcomb."

"It is always a good idea to convince people that you are a good for nothing. That way, they cannot be disappointed."

"I was being serious when I told you that I expected you to

make a decision about your future by the end of the gathering."

"I know," Sidney sighed. "I am fully aware that the good times cannot last forever. I suppose I have avoided responsibility for long enough."

"You have."

"Have you ever done something purely for the fun of it?"

"What would be the point of that?"

Sidney shook his head at his brother. "I know you and Ruth consider me to be a wastrel, but in my opinion, life is far too serious. It is up to each of us to seek pleasure when we can, for everything can change in a heartbeat."

"I have tried to find her," Henry said quietly.

"I know you have. I was not actually referring to that, but just that life is precious and can be short; our loss affects you more than me."

"I wish you had memories of her. She was a good person."

Neither needed to explain who they were talking about. Both ached in different ways for what they had lost when their mother had left.

"That does not explain why she has remained hidden since his death." Sidney stood and moved to the window. The view from the study was not as impressive as in other rooms, but Henry knew that being able to see the outdoors soothed his brother's overwhelming feeling of needing to escape. In fact, Henry was sure his brother would have left the room if he could have. After all, he was one who avoided talking about their past the most.

"There must be a good reason she has stayed away." Henry suspected he knew what that reason was, but it would do no one any good to voice it.

"And it is probably better that we do not know it."

"She did not have a choice in what happened. I know it had to have broken her heart to leave us."

"Words like that convince me that you are a hopeless romantic at heart. Go ahead, shoot daggers at me." Sidney smiled. "But I dare you to deny that you are hoping for a fairytale ending for us all."

Henry rolled his eyes. "If you are going to spout nonsense, you can leave me be. I have work to do."

Moving from the window, Sidney continued to smile. "I hope you give the people you've invited here a chance. You never know—you might actually like one or two of them and make some friendships, if nothing else. Your circle is too small. If you had more friends, there would be more chance of you enjoying your life a little."

"With men like Daniels staying? I can do without people like him in my life." That Henry had initially thought of Isabelle was soon pushed out of his mind.

"His pockets are deep, and he wants to be accepted by the *ton*. There is no harm in letting him be a part of my adventures."

"He is a bully, so I would suggest that there is indeed harm in associating with him."

"There is no need to worry. When I break the news to him that my brother has put paid to any further balloon adventures, he will not be happy at all and will probably leave, cursing me to the devil for the fact that he will not be accepted into society more widely than he has. Although he has money, he has nothing else to recommend him and you know how society views anyone who is trying to worm their way in. I foolishly thought it would be easier than it has proved to be, but believe me when I say that I have tried. I always do my best to keep my side of the bargain, but it is his own actions that have hindered his acceptance, not mine. It will be the end of a not very happy acquaintanceship."

"Good. I have never liked him, but after today, seeing the brutish way he was with his wife and the horrible manner in which he spoke to Miss Carrington, I want him off the property as soon as possible."

"Miss Carrington? I have not yet had the pleasure. Should I keep my distance if she has piqued your interest?"

"Hardly!" Henry laughed. "She is not my type." But he knew he was lying. Not meeting his brother's gaze, he was able to hide the flicker of something he had felt when seeing Isabelle challenge a man more than twice her size. He refused to admit to himself that he had been attracted to her; it was possibly admiration or something else. He inwardly shrugged, trying to dismiss that she had stirred *something* within him. Whatever it was, it was none of his brother's business.

"Oh well, it was worth a try."

"Be gone, you reprobate."

Hearing Sidney's laughter as he walked down the hallway brought a smile to Henry's lips. He was always glad to see his brother's zest for life. It gave him hope that that when the truth came out, it would not set Sidney back once more. Before his father's death, they had all suffered from dark days, but Sidney had suffered the most. And he was likely *going* to suffer the most, regardless of what Henry did. Ruth was right to suggest that Henry was trying to make up for that, but it was the right time for Sidney to establish himself and show the world he was a decent, respectable man in his own right. Henry would try to protect him as long as he could, but Sidney needed to have made connections and relationships of his own.

WALKING INTO A crowded drawing room of strangers was always especially difficult for Isabelle. No matter how often she did it, her heart would pound, hands sweat and cheeks flush as she tried to avoid the glances aimed in her direction.

It was not imagination on her part. In a society which prided itself on conformity, anything or anyone out of the ordinary was treated to stares and whispers, making them wish for the ability to fade into the background. Isabelle was an expert at avoiding attention once she was in a room, but that first entrance could not be avoided, especially when Eliza had insisted that they should be some of the last guests to arrive, so they could parade in front of everyone already gathered. Her words had set Isabelle's teeth on edge in panic, but as always, she had gone along with Eliza's demands.

She wore a dress of pale green, edged with cream scallops. Her blond hair was piled on top of her head, but she had more curls than usual falling about her face. Vainly, she thought the style softened her features, and she could hide behind the curls when she bowed her head.

Mr. Carrington squeezed Isabelle's hand as it rested on his arm, sensing her discomfort. Greeting Ruth, Edwin and Henry warmly, he and the rest of the group smoothly moved near a friend of Mr. Carrington's who was also accompanying his granddaughters.

The women were introduced and uttered pleasantries, and one, a Miss Diane Ratcliffe, smiled at Isabelle. "I have had the pleasure of hearing you sing once before. I hope I will hear you again on this visit."

"Thank you." Isabelle cursed the flush on her cheeks; the embarrassment just made her feel even hotter than she did normally. "I think Mrs. Parkinson would like me to sing at some point."

"Good," Diane responded. "This is going to be an enjoyable gathering, don't you think?"

"I hope so. I am certainly looking forward to seeing the balloon ascending."

"I can hardly believe it. I have yet to see the spectacle. Mr. Brook said he will take us to have a close look at everything as they prepare."

"I have seen one in Vauxhall Gardens, but to be able to touch the balloon is a treat indeed," Sophia said.

"As long as you do not try and get in the basket when we set off," came the teasing voice of Sidney as he approached them. "Ladies, my brother is too busy talking about the price of wheat to perform introductions, so I am left to seek out your company alone."

Isabelle's grandfather performed the introductions, and Sidney remained with them for a few moments before moving to the next group.

"He is so dashing," Diane whispered to Isabelle.

"As the second son, his prospects will be limited," Eliza interjected before Isabelle could answer.

"Eliza! We are hardly in a position to have an opinion on something like that," Isabelle hissed.

"He will hardly be a pauper," Diane said, defending the dashing young man, who was definitely the most handsome one in the room.

"It is not unreasonable to err on the side of caution," Eliza insisted. "Be friendly with Mr. Brook, but you would be wise to assess all who are here before setting your cap at him."

"Simply making one comment about him is not setting my cap at him. I would never act so gauche," Diane said stiffly. "Oh look, we are moving into supper. How very welcome."

Isabelle closed her eyes, shoulders sagging. Sophia took hold of Isabelle's arm. "Did she say what I think she said? She was open about dismissing the brother of our host to a stranger and acknowledging that she was carefully assessing every man here?"

"She will get us thrown out before the evening is over if she continues in this vein."

Sophia chuckled. "In that case, we need to keep some distance between us, as I am eager to remain here. This house is amazing."

Noticing the glare aimed in her direction by Mr. Daniels, Isabelle inwardly groaned. It seemed Eliza was not the only one who had upset a new acquaintance.

The party entered the dining room, all eager to be seated, when their attention was drawn to Mr. Daniels. "My wife is to be seated next to me," he snapped, holding the chair next to his own.

Mrs. Daniels was blushing furiously and whispered something to her husband.

"You expect me to sit and watch whilst you fawn over some

jackanape or other? I would lock you in your room first and let you starve."

Though the room had fallen silent at his outburst, no one intervened until Ruth bustled over to him, flashing a look towards Henry.

"Mr. Daniels, would it not be a tedious evening if we were all sat near our husbands and wives? I know my own Edwin is always glad of a few hours reprieve from me."

"If you are a managing woman, I can understand why he would. But Mrs. Daniels will speak to me and me alone."

Edwin and Henry both looked as if to explode at the man's impolite words, but Ruth put her hand out to stop them. Without even looking in their direction, she had sensed the reaction the words caused. "In that case, of course she can sit beside you." Ruth smiled apologetically to the woman who should have sat on Mr. Daniels's right, even though the guest looked relieved not to be sitting next to the boorish man for the evening. When the interruption had been sorted, everyone else took their own seats, and the babble of chatter replaced the uncomfortable silence Mr. Daniels had caused.

Isabelle was seated between two strangers, one who smiled at her whilst patting his stomach. "I expect you are looking forward to the food as much as I am. We will have to be careful, or there will be nothing left for the others if we have our way. It is nice to be sat next to someone who appreciates their food. Mr. Sutcliffe at your service, madam."

Isabelle stopped herself from crawling under the table to hide, but it was a close-run thing. She could only hope that no one else had heard his words. Unfortunately for her, throughout the entirety of the meal, Mr. Sutcliffe encouraged Isabelle to try everything, to have second helpings and berated her that she was not eating enough.

"You will not maintain a figure like that without eating your fill," he said jovially, tucking into his fourth portion of summer pudding.

As Isabelle had experienced nothing but feelings of nausea since taking her seat, she ate little and said less. She wondered why a jovial voice was almost as loud as an angry one as each time she was faced with yet another entreaty, some of the guests glanced over, drawn to Mr. Sutcliffe's encouragement for her to eat her fill. It was an utter relief when Ruth stood and took the ladies into the drawing room. She had never enjoyed an evening less, and there were quite a number to compare it against.

When the tea had been brought to the drawing room, Isabelle took the opportunity to approach Ruth. "I have a headache developing. Would you be very offended if I borrowed a book from the library and went to bed? I promise to be a better guest tomorrow."

"Of course, I would not be offended! I am sorry you are feeling unwell, for it means we will have to wait another evening before we can hear your voice."

"I would not give my best performance tonight." Isabelle smiled weakly. "And I think it only fair that your guests are not faced with a high-pitched wail."

"I imagine they have been subjected to some awful attempts in the past. I know I have. Was Mr. Sutcliffe so bad a dinner partner?" Ruth whispered so no one else would overhear.

"I think it is the long day taking its toll."

"You are very polite," Ruth said. "I promise not to seat you next to him again. I will have a tray sent to your room. You have earned a reprieve, I do beg your forgiveness."

"There is really no need, but thank you for excusing me."

Sophia offered to accompany Isabelle, but she shook her head. "No, you stay here and enjoy the evening. I will probably read a few pages and then fall asleep."

Kissing her friend and grandfather, Isabelle left the room as inconspicuously as possible. Approaching the library, she heard masculine voices beyond the open door and hesitated, unsure of whether to go in or not.

"Come, we must rejoin the guests. One day down, nine to

go," Henry said, approaching the door.

Sidney laughed. "You can be an old curmudgeon sometimes, though I understand why you think Miss Carrington is not your type; she would not do for you, far too quiet and timid. You need someone to bring you out of that shell of yours, a real neck-or-nothing girl. Never mind, Ruth has made sure there are lots more young ladies to tempt you."

"Blast you to the devil, you are twisting my words. I did not mean—Miss Carrington! I did not know you were here."

"I had sought permission from Mrs. Parkinson to choose a book, but I do not think I wish to read any longer."

"Please, Miss Carrington, what my brother said was..."

"I wish you would not utter what would probably be falsehoods. What I heard has just rounded off the day to perfection, and I can only agree with you that the one highlight is that there are only nine more days to go before we are all released. If you would excuse me, gentlemen." Isabelle turned on her heel and walked away.

Isabelle did not see Henry rubbing his hand over his face as she hurried upstairs. "One day, Sidney, that mouth of yours is going to get you into trouble, and I will not be able to get you out of it. How many more guests are you intending to offend?" he said once Isabelle was out of earshot.

"I will beg her pardon for both of us."

"I have a feeling I will need to do far more than that after what she overheard." The hurt expression on Isabelle's face and the way her voice wobbled ever so slightly would bother Henry for the rest of the evening.

Chapter Four

M R. CARRINGTON HAD felt unwell after the previous busy day, so Isabelle had offered to stay with him and forgo the outing to the balloon site. She was interested in the technical aspect of the flight but had insisted the others go and see what was going on. After being persuaded by her grandfather to leave him whilst he slept, she decided to take a walk and see if everyone was still at the balloon site. About to step on the staircase, she faltered upon seeing Mr. Daniels storm into the hallway, followed closely by his wife and Sidney.

"I have been taken for a fool!" Mr. Daniels shouted over his shoulder.

"Edgar, wait!" Sidney moved and caught Mr. Daniels's arm, but the older man shook off his hold.

"When were you going to tell me?" he demanded of Sidney.

"As soon as I had made a decision."

"You have already made the decision! You have just informed your guests there would be no more flights for you after this week."

Sidney smiled. "But I have not decided on what I am to do yet."

"Do not try to weasel your way out of this. You might act like I am stupid, but I have more about me than you give me credit for."

"I think highly of you, or I would not have been able to work with you these past months."

"I'm supposed to be grateful for you relieving me of my money, am I? That I have funded this scheme for so long now."

"Not all of it," Sidney said.

"Enough that it could go ahead. Just because you have fleeced me with a smile on your face does not make it any less reprehensible. I expect you are laughing at my foolishness when my back is turned, but no more! I know damn well that I have only been taken to the lowest level of gatherings. You really must have considered me an idiot if you thought I would not notice."

Sidney looked slightly uncomfortable at the accusation. "I did not think you anything of the sort. I took you to the places where I thought you would find people more welcoming to you."

Mr. Daniels looked as if to explode at Sidney's words, rather than be mollified. "Why you..."

"Mr. Daniels..." A voice from behind Sidney drew the group's attention. It was Peter, one of the other two men who were part of the balloon crew. He was accompanied by Henry, who took in the scene, including Isabelle's presence, but remained silent. "Please tell me you are still willing to invest in our scheme," Peter said.

"Did you know, Peter?" Mr. Daniels demanded of the newcomer. "Did you know that Sidney is reneging on his word to me?"

"No," Peter replied, flashing Sidney a look of reproach.

"I suppose I should feel grateful I am not the only one kept in the dark."

"We can find another third," Peter said.

"I am sure we can, but unless it is someone who can open doors for me, I am not interested. You and David bring with you no connections that are of any use," he said of the two others who made up the ballooning team.

Peter glowered at Mr. Daniels but said nothing.

"I beg forgiveness from both of you," Sidney said. "I could

use my wicked older brother as an excuse, but as he is here, he could beg to differ. I did not wish to mention anything until I had made a final decision. When I was showing everyone around, I became a little melancholic and spoke out of turn. I am truly sorry."

"I am leaving," Mr. Daniels said.

"Please stay," Sidney appealed. "You never know, you might have the pleasure of seeing Peter and David throw me overboard once we take off."

"Do not say that!" Mrs. Daniels exclaimed, looking in horror at her husband the moment the words left her mouth.

Mr. Daniels looked to be barely containing his fury. Isabelle wondered if he would strike his wife as he had done yesterday, but being in the company of others seemed to hold him back somewhat.

"I see how it is," he eventually ground out. "You will pay for this," he growled at Sidney. Without another word, he stormed out of the house. Mrs. Daniels choked on a sob and moved to follow her husband.

"Leave him," Sidney said quietly to her, touching her arm. "He will only lash out at you, and I cannot continue to stand by and say nothing when he punishes you constantly."

"It is his way," she sobbed.

"He is a bully." All laughter had gone from Sidney; he stood with teeth gritted and fists clenched. "I hate the way he treats you."

"You are very kind," Mrs. Daniels sniffed, trying to dry the ever-streaming tears.

"I have many faults, but I do not like seeing innocents being hurt."

"Thank you. Please excuse me, I think I will return to my room." She started up the stairs but faltered when she saw Isabelle.

When Isabelle held out her hand and smiled in sympathy, Mrs. Daniels rushed to her, almost throwing herself into Isabelle's arms.

"I cannot stand it anymore!"

"I understand, come with me." Isabelle looked at Henry, and he gave her a slight nod of approval, which she acknowledged with a tilt of her head.

Leading Mrs. Daniels to her chamber, she settled her in bed, ordered some tea and brandy and waited until she had fallen asleep. Wondering whether to remain in the room in case she was needed, Isabelle decided that she did not wish to be present when Mr. Daniels returned to his wife. She could only hope he would have calmed down by the time he was in anyone's company again.

Finding the hallway empty when she recommenced her attempt to go and look at the balloon site, she was startled when Henry stepped out of the library and spoke her name.

"Oh, my lord!" she exclaimed, her hand on her chest, half-laughing with the surprise.

"I beg your pardon," Henry said quickly. "Would you like to take a seat while you recollect yourself?"

"I think I will recover just fine," was her amused response.

"If you would not mind, Miss Carrington, I would like a moment of your time."

"Are you about to scold me for remaining at the top of the stairs when I should have done the polite thing and backtracked?"

Henry wanted to smile at the way the words were said so lightly, but there was a challenge within them too. "Not at all. Your being on hand to help Mrs. Daniels was appreciated. I would like to speak to you about last night."

"I would rather that particular incident be left alone." Isabelle stiffened at his words. "As I said last night, I would rather not hear false platitudes. I did not set out to eavesdrop, but what I heard could not be mistaken."

"But it was! Sidney was wrong with what he said."

"Do I take it that I am the type of woman that is to your taste?" Isabelle could not help a bitter laugh escaping. "I can see by the horror in your expression what you think of my suggestion. Do not worry, my lord. As I said last night, I too am counting down the days until I can leave. But in the meantime, I will make sure my grandfather enjoys himself reminiscing about the times he visited with your own grandfather. A pity his good nature was not passed down the family."

Isabelle turned away from Henry, shocked and utterly astounded that she had stood up for herself for once. That she was shaking did not matter; she had responded as she should have done so many times before. What was it about him that made her voice her feelings? She would not ever be so foolish as to consider that a man as handsome, titled and rich would look at her in any way other than to dismiss her, but his rejection had stung more than usual, and from him she could not accept flattery uttered purely to appease her. Cursing that she was attracted to a man who was repelled by her, she was glad no one would see the internal anger aimed towards herself for her own stupidity.

He did not try to stop her from leaving, and as she walked through the gardens, she calmed, feeling something that she had never experienced before. It was almost as if by standing up for herself, she had become more powerful. Perhaps being insulted removed any qualms about being polite and always trying to not draw attention to herself. If she was insulted anyway, why should she remain quiet? It was something to think about. And why should she not be attracted to a handsome man? She was normal in that regard, and though most of the ladies of their group seemed already smitten with Sidney, she was more attracted to the more withdrawn Henry. No, she would not condemn herself when her thoughts were perfectly normal. Even those who were not perfect could appreciate a man like Henry; she could be considered odd if she did not. Reassured that she was not the oddity everyone tried to convince her she was, she waved on seeing Sophia crossing the lawn towards her.

"You looked pleased with yourself. What mischief have you been up to?" Sophia asked.

"Would you believe that I have been putting someone in their place after they have insulted me?"

"Really? It is about time," Sophia responded. "I hope to see you in action one day, for I am sure to be impressed, though I do not wish for you to be insulted before that happens. Oh, here I go again, bumbling my way through," she laughed at herself.

"Oh, I am sure you would be astounded, but I am not going to get carried away. Being brave once might be all I am capable of."

"I hope not, for that twinkle in your eyes gives them even more sparkle than normal. It is nice to see."

"Strange that my looking well is caused by taking someone to task," Isabelle said, smiling even more at remembering Henry's surprised expression when she had scolded him. It was enough to almost look forward to the next time the opportunity arose.

ELIZA HAD COMPLAINED bitterly that the gentlemen of the group were not coming up to snuff, as they prepared for the evening meal.

"In what way have they upset you?" Sophia asked.

"They are more interested in the blasted balloon and hunting than being attentive and entertaining us."

"I, too, find the balloon very interesting," Sophia admitted.

"It is fine for a party to have something to show its guests, but when the men are standing around almost cooing at the thing and refusing to be distracted, it is a poor show."

Isabelle laughed. "Eliza, we can hardly expect to be the focus of their attention all the time. We will have the opportunity this evening to mix with them. It seems to be a very technical endeavour to fly a balloon, that is why they are so fascinated about it. I am sure that once they have seen it fly and especially if they manage to obtain even the smallest flight in it, they will settle down a little more. We cannot expect them to be indoors for our entertainment every day."

"You are so dismissive of me, but if it continues in this way, none of us will have secured a match before the party ends."

"We might not wish to," Sophia said.

"Then you are as much a fool as Isabelle is!"

"Eliza! Enough of your bad manners!" Isabelle exclaimed. "I will not have you casting aspersions at either of us, but particularly Sophia. Just because we do not intend to throw ourselves at the unmarried men in the group, that is no excuse to ridicule us. The way you are speaking, if your actions are so blatant, it is no wonder the men are giving you a wide berth."

"That is outrageous!" Eliza shouted. "How dare you!"

"I dare because your bad manners cannot go unchecked."

"I will go to Grandfather and tell him that he has wasted his money on bringing you here if all you are to do is dismiss opportunities." She flounced out of the room, and the friends looked at one another without speaking.

Only when the maid had left did Sophia take the opportunity to speak to Isabelle. "I like this new version of you."

"New version? That is a strange turn of phrase."

"It is the only way I can describe it. Something has changed ever since you stood up for yourself with Madame Francine."

"I could not bear the thought of not having a dress in that material. I always accept what Mother and Madame Francine decide on. For some reason, it really annoyed me that they were not listening to my wishes."

"And from the smile on your face at the memory, you quite enjoyed speaking up for yourself."

Isabelle's smile widened. "I admit it did feel good, though not so much when she was stabbing me with pins because of my insolence."

"I would definitely seek out a different modiste. Your grandfather keeps you well dressed. I am sure there are plenty who would welcome your custom."

"I have always chosen my battles carefully. I can win the occasional skirmish, but I know with regards to Mother, I would never win the war."

"I wish she did not browbeat you the way she does."

Isabelle pulled on her gloves, not looking at Sophia. "It is because I am such a disappointment to her. If she had other, normal daughters, she would not be focused on my faults quite so much."

"I hate it when you speak so. You are a lovely person; I just wish you would believe it."

"But I am most certainly not his lordship's type." Isabelle was still hurt by their exchanges, but she could take some amusement from the shock on Henry's face when she had asked him for clarification.

"Then he is a nodcock."

"Of course, he is. Let us join Eliza and Grandfather. She is wishing to perform tonight."

"Oh Lord! Does Mrs. Parkinson understand that singing ability does not run in your family?"

"Sophia!"

"I am speaking the truth! You cannot scold me for that."

"It is bad manners," Isabelle chided.

"No. It is a fact."

Chapter Five

RUTH HAD BEEN true to her word and sat Isabelle far away from Mr. Sutcliffe the following evening. He had waved at Isabelle, but though she smiled back, she had quickly turned to her own dinner partners. She was seated between Sidney and Peter. There seemed to be a tense atmosphere between the two gentlemen, which she put down to what happened earlier in the day.

Sidney leaned closer to Isabelle. "I am glad you are here to protect me from my friend Boyd," he said of Peter. "If his glowers are anything to go by, I will be tipped out of the balloon."

"You could spend your time working out how we can persuade Daniels to continue funding us," Peter muttered across Isabelle to Sidney. "He is threatening that after this week, we will not get a penny more."

"He is all bluster. He will come around," Sidney said before turning his attention to the lady sitting at his other side.

Breaking the silence, Isabelle smiled at Peter. "I was sorry to miss the talk you gave earlier."

"Perhaps after our first flight tomorrow, I could give you a tour."

"Are you intending to fly so soon? I thought it would take days before we saw a flight."

"As we will be forced to sell everything once our main backer goes, I would like to make as many flights as we can this week."

"It must be very freeing, being above everything, with only you and the birds in the sky." Isabelle was doing her best to try and distract him but was not sure that speaking about the balloon was the right topic, given the circumstances.

She was relieved when her words caused a change in him, all sullenness leaving his features and a smile lighting up his face. "It is like nothing else, the peace, the absolute reliance on the wind and your own ability to keep you in the sky. I cannot describe how alive it makes one feel."

"I think you are doing a fine job of it. You make me quite jealous."

"If everything goes to plan, we could arrange for some of the guests to be lifted off the ground. We would need a lot of help to keep the lines tethered, but it would give everyone an idea of what it feels like."

"That would be wonderful! It is very good of you to think of us all."

"I am to be the first," Mr. Daniels said from diagonally across the table, completely ignoring etiquette.

"Of course," Peter said through gritted teeth. "We would never dare to do it any other way."

"Aye, well, it is about time I got some benefit for my investment."

"We have tried to be frugal in every way we could."

"I beg to differ. If I took a close look at your accounts, I am sure there would be some questionable spending."

"Are you accusing me of dishonesty?" Peter clenched his fists, which had been resting on the table.

"Did I mention your name?" Mr. Daniels sneered. "It sounds like you have a guilty conscience the way you are reacting."

"How dare you aim such a slur in my direction! You are not only withdrawing your funds but are ensuring we will not be able to attract funding from anyone else." Pushing his chair back, Peter stood. "I have had enough of this! Keep your damned money, but I will not let you get away with suggesting that I am dishonest. I should put a bullet through you for that."

"Enough!" Henry demanded from the head of the table, glaring at both men.

Peter stormed out of the room. A few moments later, the shocked silence was broken by Mr. Daniels. "I am glad this is to be the end of our agreement, Sidney. I do not like the men you associate with."

Sidney looked thunderous at the comment, but before he could reply, Henry stood. "Mr. Daniels, a word." Walking out without waiting for a reply, Henry left the furious Mr. Daniels no choice but to follow him.

Ruth stood and led the ladies out of the room. Mrs. Daniels had hung back, clearly distressed by what had happened and seeming unsure of what to do. Eliza was busy whispering to an older woman she had taken a shine to, which suited Isabelle and Sophia, for they preferred to offer help without Eliza's interference.

They approached Mrs. Daniels. "If you would like to join us, you would be more than welcome," Sophia said.

"I do not know what to do," Mrs. Daniels whispered, wringing her hands.

"Mr. Daniels did not mind you retiring with the ladies last night. He will know where to find you," Isabelle said.

"It is so difficult to always do the right thing, to not upset him." Seeming to suddenly recollect herself, her hand covered her mouth in horror.

Isabelle smiled, linking arms with Mrs. Daniels and walking out of the dining room. "Do not fret. Your secret is safe with us. I think we all have relatives who we sometimes consider a little testing, shall we say." She looked pointedly at her cousin.

For the first time since her arrival, Mrs. Daniels smiled. "Yes, it can be difficult."

"In that case, let us enjoy our slight reprieve." Seating themselves to one side in the elegant drawing room, the threesome did not join in with the larger group.

"You must have seen so many balloon ascensions that you are bored with them by now," Sophia said, changing the subject.

"Oh no! I rarely get the opportunity to see any. Mr. Daniels does not like me coming to any events. He says I will make a blunder and embarrass him."

Isabelle and Sophia shared a look, but it was Sophia who spoke. "You fit in perfectly from the little I have seen of you."

"Thank you, that is very kind, but my family made their fortune in trade, and I know how that is frowned on."

"Only by the stupid ones in society," Isabelle said.

Mrs. Daniels laughed, the sound seeming to surprise her as much as it did Isabelle and Sophia. "I wish all were like you, though Mr. Daniels would probably ban me from speaking to you. He does not like it when women have their own ideas."

"I am sure he does not," Isabelle said dryly. "Forgive my impertinence, but is there a large age difference between you?"

"Yes, twenty years. Mr. Daniels convinced my father that in order to gain improvement, I would need someone with his experience and ability to get on in the world."

"How long have you been married?" Sophia asked.

"Four years. We wed as soon as I turned sixteen. I told my father that I was quite happy helping out in the business, but he said I should be grateful to have the opportunity to better myself."

"You were so young," Isabelle murmured.

"I am not a lot of use as a wife, though." Eyes downcast, she started to wring her hands once more. "Mr. Daniels is not happy that we have not had children yet. He thinks I am being barren on purpose."

The gentlemen entered the room at that moment, providing a welcome diversion, as Mrs. Daniels failed to notice the shocked and disgusted expressions her words caused. Henry and Mr. Daniels were still missing.

"He will be so angry," Mrs. Daniels muttered to herself, noticing her husband's absence.

Sidney approached the threesome, his smile in place. "Ladies, you are seated to perfection. All the other ladies must be jealous to be out-dazzled by you."

Mrs. Daniels giggled and flushed whilst Sophia and Isabelle laughed.

"I expect you say that to every group you approach," Isabelle said.

"Not at all!" But his laugh undermined his words. "Mrs. Daniels, ladies, would you give me permission to bring you your tea? It would be a shame for you to be disturbed when you make such a pretty picture."

"Of course," Mrs. Daniels answered, flushing even more when Sidney took her hand and kissed it.

Bringing a cup for Mrs. Daniels first, he presented it with a flourish and an exaggerated bow. "Ladies, I shall return with your refreshments." Bowing to Isabelle and Sophia, he moved away.

He paused in confusion when Mrs. Daniels gasped and turned to see a resigned-looking Henry and a furious Mr. Daniels standing in the doorway. Nodding to them both, he returned to the table of tea items as if nothing was amiss.

Performing the same flourishing delivery, he then sat next to Isabelle. "I think I need to offer my protection if the glowers aimed in this direction are anything to go by," he said with a gesture towards Mr. Daniels, who had been waylaid in his approach to their group.

"As most of the black looks seem to be aimed at you, I think it is us who are offering you protection," Isabelle responded, smiling at the laugh her words caused.

"You are a bad influence, Miss Carrington. Now my brother is glaring daggers at me."

Henry was staring at them both intently, but just when they thought he would approach them, he moved over to Ruth, whispering something in her ear. Nodding to him, Ruth stood and approached the group.

"Miss Carrington, could I impose on you to start our musical interlude this evening?"

"Well—I—yes, if you insist." Isabelle was surprised that she was the first one to be approached.

"Thank you. I agree with Henry's suggestion that we need some light entertainment this evening." Ruth did not look at Mr. Daniels, who had moved to stand behind his wife, eyes boring into her.

"I am happy to perform for you, Mrs. Parkinson. You just need to say the word," Eliza said, seeming to appear from nowhere.

"Of course," Ruth said, disguising the fact that Eliza had startled her. "If you would like to follow your cousin."

"If that is what you wish, but as the elder of the two of us, I do rank higher than Isabelle. In many ways, in fact."

"I am more than happy to have Eliza perform first," Isabelle responded.

"You are very good," Ruth said, her tone stiffening when she spoke to Eliza. "The piano is all yours, Miss Hodge."

Eliza looked triumphantly at Isabelle before moving to the piano.

"Why does she consider everything as a competition between you both?" Sophia asked.

"I have no idea, to be honest. She has been like this for as long as I can remember."

Eliza started to play, and though proficient, her air was that of someone who considered herself a superior musician, but the audience was inclined to wince when the obvious mistakes were made.

When two songs had been performed, Ruth moved to Eliza, thanking her for a wonderful recital and invited Isabelle to join her.

"Would you like me to play for you, Miss Carrington? Your grandfather informed me that you prefer not to play and sing."

"You really have done your research." Isabelle smiled. "But

he is correct, so I would certainly take you up on your kind offer."

"I like to do all I can to help my guests be comfortable."

Isabelle stood to the side of the instrument, using it as a shield almost. She let her hands straighten her dress, a deep green which warmed her complexion and complemented her hair perfectly.

Henry had remained at the back of the room when he had returned with Mr. Daniels. As Isabelle and Ruth decided on songs, Sidney approached him. "Did you sort out Daniels?"

"I thought I had, until we entered the room and found you mooning over his wife," Henry said.

"I was hardly doing that!"

"She looked happier gazing at you than she has at any other point in her stay."

"I was just trying to show her a little kindness."

"You cannot save others, just like we could do nothing to help Mother. I know you always want to help those who remind you of her situation."

"Blast you! It is not always about her," Sidney ground out. "You are more affected than I with regards to that. You forget I was a babe in arms when it all happened."

"My mistake. But you could have chosen your moment better."

"I am glad my association with him is coming to an end. I have never spent so much time with him until now, and I am rapidly beginning to detest the man."

"A pity you did not discover it before you invited him here. Oh!" The exclamation had been uttered involuntarily the moment Isabelle had started to sing.

The whole room stilled as Isabelle changed from the slightly withdrawn, attention-avoiding spinster to a woman with a voice that could not be ignored. From the spellbound expressions on everyone's face, the whole audience was enraptured.

When the first song came to an end, there was resounding applause and shouts for more, causing Isabelle to flush, but she nodded her agreement to Ruth.

"Isn't she a surprise?" Sidney asked, joining in with the calls for an encore.

"She has surprised me on a few occasions," Henry answered. "She is not what I thought on first meeting her."

"Oh really?" Sidney chuckled.

"Do not be ridiculous. I would expect Ruth to insinuate in that way, not you, or I might start to make further assumptions about you and Mrs. Daniels."

"Touché," Sidney muttered good-naturedly, but they both fell silent the moment Isabelle started to sing once more.

Henry was glad he had been able to divert Sidney because he did not wish to confess how Isabelle had managed to creep under his skin. It had started from the first moment he had seen her take Mr. Daniels to task. The fire in her eyes and the way she had stood up to a man twice her size had been impressive and amusing.

But then he had insulted her.

That had been unforgivable and made his skin crawl with embarrassment. He was not a cruel man, and seeing the hurt in her expression had shamed him. But the way she had reacted with such dignity in standing up for herself had almost brought him to his knees in his need to beg forgiveness.

Now she sounded like an angel, and he was having a hard time keeping his eyes averted from the smooth, creamy skin of her throat; all he could think of was how it would feel to kiss that tender skin. The way he was responding to her was unexpected and concerning. He had too much of his father in him, at least that was his constant fear, and he could never in all conscience inflict himself on such a good soul. He remembered some of the pain his father had inflicted on his mother, not all, but enough that he would sometimes wake from a nightmare, sweaty and heart-pumping, thinking he could hear the sound of fist on skin. Yes, he had denied any attraction to Sidney, but he would hardly reveal an attraction to Isabelle to his brother. Sidney would torment him until he wished Isabelle miles away, but he could acknowledge she was an intriguing, enticing package.

It would not do to get carried away, though, reminding himself that he would have to be content with admiring from afar. Anything else was wasted energy, for he would not allow any closeness between them; he was far too damaged and too much aware of what could lurk in his character if he were to become like his father. It was a real fear he held, for surely his father must have been different in his younger days. It was essential that he not become attached to anyone, in case he developed in the same way he presumed his father had.

Though there were no signs to cause him even more concern, every time he was annoyed, every time he felt anger bubbling within him, he would wonder if this was it–if the monster was finally coming to the surface. It was an unbearable thought which caused him physical pain. He had hated his father, especially for the fears the man had instilled in him, preventing him from having a happy future.

Not for the first time in his life, he cursed that his mother had ever met his father.

Chapter Six

E VERYONE WAS EXCITED at the start of the new day. Even those who usually chose to linger in their bedchamber had ventured down to the breakfast room. Breakfast was being served earlier than normal, as the balloonists had said that the wind was better the earlier they could start.

As guests started to leave the room to make their way to the outside viewing area, which had been set up with tables, chairs and blankets, there was a commotion in the hallway.

Mr. and Mrs. Daniels had been the only two absent at breakfast, and as they came downstairs, it was clear why. Mrs. Daniels was sporting a black eye that even a thick dusting of powder could not disguise. Sidney had been crossing the hall, all joviality about the coming flight until he had glanced up as he passed the stairs and saw them.

Only stilling for a moment, he charged up the stairs, grabbed Mr. Daniels by his frock coat and dragged him down the last few steps. "You damned cur! I am going to kill you for hurting her!" Sidney threw punch after punch until Henry and Edwin jumped into the fray and pulled Sidney away from the prone man.

Mrs. Daniels had run to her husband, falling to her knees next to him and checking him over while constantly begging his forgiveness.

"You are asking for his pardon?" Sidney asked incredulously.

"It is my fault that I bruise so easily," Mrs. Daniels answered, hardly glancing at Sidney. "You attacked him for no reason."

Sidney indicated to Edwin and Henry that it was safe to let him go. He still looked furious but more in control of himself. "I suggest you look at his actions before starting to aim accusations in my direction."

"You cannot save her if she does not wish to be saved," Henry said quietly.

"For once, brother, we are in total agreement," Sidney said before storming out of the house without a backward glance.

"Your brother is a brute," Mr. Daniels said, trying to stand but struggling. "I need my cane!"

Mrs. Daniels ran to the hall stand in which the canes were kept, grabbed the long-handled, silver-tipped one that Mr. Daniels used and handed it to her husband.

"We are leaving after we see this flight," he said to his wife. "And you can stop those tears before they start. I want no more of them."

"I understand," Mrs. Daniels choked and, pulling on her gloves, she followed her husband out of the house.

Henry and Edwin looked at each other and grimaced. "I suppose the only bright side is that Daniels seems determined to leave," Edwin said.

"I will still need to speak to Sidney about his hero complex," Henry muttered.

"He is not the only one in the family with one of those," Edwin responded with a raised eyebrow.

"It is a fine quality, though misplaced," Eliza's voice came from behind the two gentlemen.

Both men swung around in surprise, emotions too raw to hide the glare aimed at Eliza, but she continued, oblivious to their annoyance at her rudeness.

"He should be careful showing so much inclination to a married woman. Gossip can spread, and as Mrs. Daniels's background is in trade, her reputation would not stand a scandal."

"None of our reputations would if we were foolish enough to upset the wrong people," Isabelle said, grabbing Eliza by the arm and propelling her towards the outer door.

"Unhand me, Isabelle! What on earth has come over you?"

"The distinct urge to commit murder," Isabelle ground out. Hearing the men chuckle made her flush that they had overheard her words.

Eliza managed to shake Isabelle off, but only when they had reached the outside of the house. "How dare you interfere with my person in such a brutish way! I am quite disgusted with you."

"I would not even ask what my opinion is of you at this time, for it would not be a pleasant exchange," Isabelle retorted.

"I am not interested in the slightest."

"A pity. Because if you keep on in this vein, Mr. Daniels will not be the only one leaving this afternoon, even if I have to feign hysterics to convince Grandfather we need to return home."

"You would not!"

"Try me, Eliza. Unless you start acting with decorum, I refuse to have my reputation damaged because of your actions."

"This is preposterous! You cannot dictate what we do."

"Speak to Grandfather if you think I am wrong."

"He will support you, he always does, when we all know the reason he indulges you."

"And what reason is that?" Isabelle asked. Her voice was dangerously low as the cousins faced each other, completely unaware that they were attracting curious looks from those who were now leaving the house to watch the balloon ascent.

"He spoils you because he knows that no matter how hard you try, you will always be unmarried because of the size of you."

Isabelle took a step towards Eliza, the same fire in her eyes that Henry had been witness to when she stood up to Mr. Daniels. The fury in the glare had Eliza rooted to the spot, eyes widening in shock. "You, Eliza, are a bully, and I will not stand for it a moment longer. I am overweight, fat even, but that does not give you or anyone else the right to judge me or make comments. I am sick of putting up with bad manners and personal insults, especially from those who would benefit from giving their own actions as much scrutiny as they give mine." Isabelle was breathing heavily, eyes wide, but she flushed a deep pink.

From behind, the sound of clapping made her spin around. Ruth and Sophia were standing together in the doorway, both applauding.

"This is nothing to be happy about," Isabelle said mortified.

"I disagree," Ruth said. "It is unfair that you are punished so when we all have faults, some more than others."

Eliza turned on her heel and stomped away without another word, refusing to look at anyone.

"I know my question is impertinent, but why does she dislike you so much?" Ruth asked.

"Jealousy," Sophia said without hesitation. "But she is getting worse."

Isabelle snorted. "As if there is anything about me for her to be jealous about."

Ruth tsked. "You will never receive respect from anyone if you do not respect yourself."

"It is hard to do that after a lifetime of being told one thing; you are suddenly expected to forget what has gone on in the past and become something or someone you have no experience of being."

"Ah, the past, that is somewhere my brothers and I would rather forget, but I agree it is sometimes hard to do so," Ruth said, with a glance to the house as if remembering something she would rather not. "Come. Enough of this maudlin mood! The balloon must be ready by now!"

The women moved off together, not noticing Henry and Edwin leaving the house when they had moved away.

"I wish I had answers for Ruth, for us all," Henry said as they followed the group. "She tries to dismiss it, making light of it, but I know it affects her as it does Sidney and me."

"She has nightmares about it still," Edwin said.

"Does she? Damn it, I must make more of an effort. I will arrange for more resources to be made available. We need answers."

"As I have said to Ruth, you might not like what you find."

"I think in trying to protect Sidney, I have neglected Ruth's needs."

"Do not forget about yourself. You must have as many questions as Ruth has."

"I have, but I think not wishing to stir up the past has made me less inclined to find out the truth, since Father died anyway. I should not have considered myself above their needs, for I know they both struggle in different ways."

"You are a good brother to them both."

Henry smiled. "I doubt Sidney would think that if I did indeed force him into the regulars."

Henry and Edwin approached some of the company, who sat at the tables which had been positioned to cater for their older guests. They were in the line of sight of the balloon but far enough away that they could enjoy the spectacle without needing to move out of the way of any of the activity. There was another group who had gathered in the field with the balloon, the seated guests overlooking them. Everyone was keeping well back from the large structure but had huddled together, wishing to be as close as possible without being at risk from the unpredictable balloon.

Sidney, Peter and David were already in the balloon basket, and farmhands were keeping it secure with a number of ropes. The balloon was not fully inflated, but it was still an extraordinary sight, with the crimson and gold silk undulating in the breeze. It was clear to everyone that it was straining to escape its tethers as the farmhands struggled to keep it grounded. The strength and feeling of it almost being a live thing had the audience looking at it in wonder, eager to see it in its full glory.

"Any longer and you would have missed it," Mr. Carrington

said to Henry. He was seated next to a very sullen Eliza.

"It looks impressive. I can understand why Sidney is enthralled by it," Henry said.

"He reminds me of a younger version of your grandfather," Mr. Carrington said. "Always looking for the next thing to try."

"Did he ever settle down?" Henry asked with a raised eyebrow.

Mr. Carrington chuckled. "Eventually."

"There is hope then."

"I would like to get closer," Edwin said, and they moved away from Mr. Carrington.

Unable to stop himself from seeking out Isabelle, Henry could not help a smile touching his lips as he watched her excitement as she gathered with the others, chatting and pointing out anything new. She was not the most gregarious of people, but there was something quietly vibrant about her. She seemed to take pleasure in life, and he could only envy that.

Seeing her so animated made her even more attractive to him. The sudden thought made him take a sharp breath, and his smile was replaced by a frown. Even more attractive? Since when had he begun to think of her in that way? When had he started to seek her out in a crowd, needing to know where she was?

Trying not to let anyone see that he was troubled by his thoughts, he silently groaned. He had felt a pull towards her the second time he had seen her, though it was one thing to be attracted to a woman, and something completely different to be interested in only her. That suggested his feelings went beyond simple appreciation, which was a disturbing thought that he would have to overcome.

He returned his attention to the balloon in some surprise; he had been so focused on Isabelle that he had missed the large beastlike structure lifting from the ground, where it hung restlessly, still tethered by its ropes but pulling against them. He needed to take control of this distracting nonsense, for it would not do. He had made an informed decision about his future—the right decision. Only now was it beginning to feel like the lonely choice.

Forcing his eyes on the balloon, he only looked back to where Isabelle was standing when there was sudden movement, and a shout of exclamation from one of the guests. The sound indicated that something was seriously wrong, and his stomach turned at the possibility that Isabelle could be in danger...and he had not protected her.

Moving quickly, he paused only for a second when he saw Isabelle was fine. Some of the tension left his body at that revelation. But what had happened? Unable to guess what was going on, he moved towards the group, and, arriving, he saw Mr. Daniels lying on the ground.

"Blast it," he muttered, picking up speed. "Who has he upset now?"

THERE WAS A party atmosphere in the group that had formed at the edge of the field. Isabelle had finally managed to put behind her what had been exchanged at the house. After all, there was no point repining when everyone, including her, was excited to see the ascension.

All the younger members of the house party were gathered, a few rolling their eyes when Mr. Daniels joined them, but as everyone was aware that he was funding the project, no one could begrudge him wishing to be close to the action. As always, Mrs. Daniels hovered by his side. She regularly asked him if there was anything he needed or if he would like something to sit on.

"I am not in my dotage," he eventually snapped at her. "I am more than capable of standing for ten minutes."

"I just want you to enjoy yourself," Mrs. Daniels responded in her usual pitiful way.

"In that case, speak when you are spoken to; otherwise, shut up!"

Mrs. Daniels was silent for a few moments and then sniffed, wiping her eyes with her handkerchief.

"Oh, for goodness sake. Get me a drink if you need to do something, and dry your tears," Mr. Daniels snapped, slamming his cane in a fit of temper several times on the ground in time with his words. It was embarrassing to witness: Mrs. Daniels once again being treated shabbily by her husband, and those around them moving away a little in discomfort.

Luckily, at that point, the balloon started to rise, and the group moved forward in excitement, jostling against each other, closer than they would be normally.

Mr. Daniels let out a grunt, and Mrs. Daniels immediately asked him once more if he needed anything. When he did not answer, she moved closer to him, seeming to go towards his front before pulling back a little.

"I will get you that drink now," she said, her voice higher than usual.

Isabelle had been close enough to hear the exchange, and though her blood boiled at the way Mr. Daniels spoke to his wife, she said and did nothing to inflame the situation further. She was coming to the conclusion that no one could assist Mrs. Daniels until the woman asked for help, and she was not sure she ever would. Mrs. Daniels seemed to be resigned to her fate, which was a pity, for her husband was a cruel man.

Turning when she heard Mrs. Daniels squeak out her last words, she wondered what Mr. Daniels could have possibly said to cause the look of pure terror on his wife's face.

Isabelle forced herself not to follow Mrs. Daniels as she scurried across the grass and eventually turned back to watch the balloon's ascension.

"Do you mind?" Diane uttered to Mr. Daniels, who was leaning on her in a most inappropriate way.

Getting no response to her question, Diane moved in an effort to force some distance between them. When Mr. Daniels fell face-down, jostling a few others as he crumpled to the ground, she let out an exclamation of shock, attracting gasps from everyone else in the group.

It felt to Isabelle that Henry arrived almost immediately. He looked closely at her before turning to where Mr. Daniels lay. A young man was already crouched by Mr. Daniels's side.

"Has he taken ill?" Henry asked. "Does he need a doctor?"

"He is beyond help, my lord," the gentleman said.

"Has he had a heart attack?" Sophia asked.

"I do not think so," the gentleman replied, a frown in place as he attempted to roll the bulky man over in an effort to work out what had happened.

"Miss Ratcliffe, look at your pelisse," another member of the group, a Mr. Corless, said to Diane.

Diane looked at the pale green pelisse and started to pat at it, as if she could make what she had seen disappear.

"Is that blood?" Sophia asked on a whisper.

"It would seem so," Isabelle replied, moving to Diane. "Miss Ratcliffe, I will help, please be still."

"I did not know he was injured," Diane cried to Isabelle. "He must have taken ill, and I did not help him."

"You could not have done anything to help him," Mr. Corless said, nodding to where Mr. Daniels had been rolled onto his back. Staining on his waistcoat was visible when Mr. Corless undid Mr. Daniels's frock coat. Blood was still trickling from a hole just under his ribs, the wound barely visible except for the frayed material around the rent. "I would say he has been stabbed. The wound is not round and we would have heard a pistol being fired. However it was achieved, it seems he has been murdered."

"Oh my God!" Diane uttered before crumpling into a dead faint.

Chapter Seven

"**H**AS SOMEONE GOT smelling salts?" Isabelle asked, immediately crouching beside Diane and rubbing the young woman's hands. She was passed a small bottle, and before using it, she heard Henry curse.

Mrs. Daniels was running towards them. Henry tried to intercept her, but she managed to side-step him. Seeing her husband on the ground, clearly dead, she put her hands to her face and started to scream. Isabelle could only glance at the distraught woman before turning back to Diane.

When Diane was finally conscious—though in tears, it did not seem that she would faint again—Isabelle left her side to ask two of the ladies—who seemed to wish themselves far away but were unable to move—if they would escort Diane back to the house. Seeming relieved to be given instructions, they helped Diane to stand and led her away from the scene.

Everyone who had joined the group looked lost, as if not quite sure as what to do. It was natural but Isabelle knew now was not the time to freeze, or succumb to the horror of the situation. She had to be practical.

Isabelle turned with a wince at the noise Mrs. Daniels was uttering as she continued to scream. Henry was calmly trying to get her to listen to him, but her eyes were glazed, seemingly fixed on her husband's body.

Isabelle felt nauseous, unable to look away from the wound and blood on Mr. Daniels's body. She had never seen anything like it, and glancing at Sophia, she saw the same look of horror she imagined she wore. No one seemed to know what to do, almost as if time had stopped the moment they had discovered Mr. Daniels was dead.

Shaking herself out of her stupor, she looked to Henry, who was still trying to speak to Mrs. Daniels. "We need to move everyone away," she said. It felt natural that she had instinctively turned to Henry and not just because he was the head of the house.

"Could you try and help Mrs. Daniels?" Henry asked her, immediately responding to her words. "Ruth, take the others to the house and settle everyone down."

Ruth had appeared after Henry had, followed closely by Edwin. "I will send footmen to help," Ruth said.

"There is no need." Henry nodded towards the house where several servants were coming towards them.

"I will help secure the balloon," Edwin said, striding to join the farmhands who were already steadying the barely-risen balloon. Though the three men on board were working to land the contraption, their faces were serious, glances aimed towards the group, which was becoming smaller as Ruth ushered people back to the house.

"Miss Carrington, Miss Belmont, could I ask that you escort Mrs. Daniels, please? I know you have been kind towards her, and I feel she would respond better to you than anyone else. We will deal with Mr. Daniels when she is gone," Henry said.

"Certainly," Isabelle and Sophia said, though they hesitantly stepped beyond the body of Mr. Daniels. The surprised expression they saw on his face felt macabre, and the smell of blood made them both swallow convulsively.

"Mrs. Daniels, please come with us," Sophia said.

"No! I cannot leave him, he needs help! Why is the doctor not here?"

Exchanging a look with Sophia, Isabelle stood next to the sobbing woman and put her arm around her. "No one can help him now, but he would want you to be cared for. Please come with us; it would be better if you were in the house."

"No! I need to be with him! I don't know what to do; he always told me what to do."

"He did, and if he was able to, he would be telling you to dry your tears and go back to the house." Isabelle kept her voice gentle and calm, knowing that Henry would not move Mr. Daniels until his wife was out of sight.

Mrs. Daniels hiccupped. "He hated that I cried all the time."

"I do not think he would mind at the moment, but we do need to return to the house. I am sure he would agree."

"I don't want to leave him!"

"He would not wish to be lying on the grass, would he? They can only move him if you leave," Isabelle continued, her tone gentle but firm.

"He hated the outdoors, said it was unhealthy."

Isabelle could not think of a comment to give in response to that. Her initial reaction was that Mr. Daniels had been right in that regard, but as quickly as the thought entered her mind, she cursed her insensitivity. She helped Mrs. Daniels to stand, and when Sophia took Mrs. Daniels's other arm, they half-carried her back to the house. Isabelle was unsure if she actually registered what they were doing.

Sidney, Peter and David all rushed over to Henry once the balloon was secured. The footmen had covered the body in sheets and were carrying it up to the house by the time the three arrived.

"What on earth happened?" Sidney demanded. "Was it heart failure?"

"No." Henry rubbed his hand over his face. "He was stabbed, if the wound under his ribs is anything to go by."

"What?"

"Stabbed?"

"Murdered?" came the three shocked replies.

Henry nodded. "I take it from your reactions that you did not see anything?"

"To be honest, we were more concerned about the balloon ascension. There was no time to even think about what was going on beyond the ropes," Peter said. "It might look easy, but it is most certainly not."

"I suspected as much," Henry responded.

"Who would want to murder him?" David asked.

"There is probably a list of people in this house alone," Sidney said dryly.

"Yes, aren't you three glad you were some distance away?" Henry asked.

"Us? Why?" David asked.

"He was going to stop funding your adventures after this week. Some would say that is a motive."

"If he is dead, we receive no money at all and do not have the ability to persuade him otherwise," Peter snapped.

"But Mrs. Daniels is now a wealthy widow and is very keen on ballooning," Henry pointed out.

"Then lucky for us we were in full view of everyone the whole time and nowhere near her husband," Sidney said with a pointed look at his brother.

"Do not glare daggers at me; I am not saying that you are suspects. Unfortunately, however, the guests who were gathered around him in that little group most certainly are."

"Surely someone would have seen something? You cannot just stab a person when there are others around. To kill someone with a knife would need a forceful movement," Sidney said. "It is unbelievable to suggest that no one saw anything."

"If they did, I will find out, for I will be questioning them all," Henry said grimly.

"Are you sending for the constable?" Sidney asked.

"No—at least not yet. As magistrate, I am quite entitled to make my own enquiries. I will only need him once the culprit is identified."

"If you need any help, just let me know."

Henry looked in surprise at his brother. "I will. Thank you."

"There is no need to sound quite so shocked," Sidney said. "I am not a complete wastrel."

"Just a slight one?" Henry asked as they all turned towards the house.

"I refuse to answer that as it is just a question from a spiteful older brother."

"I cannot believe that you are funning when a man is dead," David said in disgust.

"Are you telling me that you are to go into mourning for him? That you are genuinely upset that you no longer have to put up with his moods and tantrums?" Sidney asked.

"Maybe not, but I do believe in showing respect for the dead," David snapped.

"I agree with David. We should be showing more respect," Peter said.

"I am sorry he has been murdered," Sidney responded. "Though it comes as no surprise. I wanted to kill him myself when I saw how he treated his wife, but I would not hang for doing such a thing. I will also not be a hypocrite. I disliked the man, but I acknowledge that no one deserves an end like that."

"Then you should stop being irreverent. You are coming across as a lofty devil-may-care nodcock," Peter said.

"Peter, there is no need for that." David backtracked at Peter's strong insult.

"Is there not? We both think it."

"I cannot believe that a throwaway comment I made to my brother has given you the right to condemn the whole of my character. I am glad to hear your true opinion of me; it makes the separation of our partnership easier to bear."

"You were always going to leave us in the lurch. Your type always does." Peter stormed off; David followed, shooting Sidney a look of apology.

"I am glad I do not have friends like those two," Henry said drily.

"As you do not have friends, you are hardly in a position to comment," Sidney retorted.

Ignoring the barb, Henry continued. "I am even happier to know you were in the balloon at the time of the murder, for either of those two would throw you to the lions if they could."

"Don't I know it. It is a good thing this is coming to an end. You were right to force my hand."

"Wonders will never cease. You agree with me."

"Do not get used to it."

"I would not be so foolish."

ISABELLE AND SOPHIA entered their room looking tired and drained. Mr. Carrington and Eliza were waiting for them.

"Come, sit down. I ordered some brandy for when you returned, so have a little now. You have both had a shock," Mr. Carrington said, leading them both to a chair.

"It was horrible," Sophia said, accepting the glass from Mr. Carrington.

"What a horrible way to die—murdered because you were hated so much," Eliza said, hand on heart.

Isabelle shot her cousin a look but said nothing, though she smiled a little when her grandfather raised his eyebrows at her.

"You two must be especially concerned now, and rightly so," Eliza continued.

"Why?" Isabelle asked.

"You were there, near the murderer. You could even be the one who killed him!"

"Do not be ridiculous," Mr. Carrington scolded his granddaughter.

"I am not! Isabelle had more than one argument with Mr.

Daniels; it is clear she did not like him."

"Disliking someone is a long way from murdering them, Eliza." Isabelle tried to keep her tone level, but the whole episode had been a shock, and her head was starting to throb now her body was relaxing as a result of the brandy.

"What has Isabelle to gain from murdering Mr. Daniels?" Sophia asked.

"He did not like that she was friendly with his wife, and the arguments between them did not show her in a good light. I have often noticed his lordship looking in her direction, very often frowning. So it is not just me who has observed the way she was with Mr. Daniels."

"That is because Lord Gosforth admires her," Sophia defended her friend. "She is the one he speaks to the most, and he seeks her out regularly."

"Probably because I argue with him, too." Isabelle managed to laugh. "Perhaps he will be my next victim?"

"You might mock me…"

"I would not dare, Eliza. I can honestly say that I have felt like murdering his lordship on more than one occasion."

Eliza looked relieved. "That is a good thing, for I did worry that you were developing ideas that would come to naught."

"Eliza!" Mr. Carrington exclaimed. "Mind your tongue, girl!"

"What have I said that is wrong? If Isabelle has set her cap at his lordship, she is to be sadly disappointed. Surely you cannot be hoping for her to make a match of it with him?"

"I would be happy if any of you managed to secure a young man," Mr. Carrington said diplomatically. "You all are worthy of the highest titles."

Isabelle smiled. "Said by a completely unbiased sweetheart."

"Of course. Grandpapa, you need to accept that his lordship will know full well what is expected of him and will act accordingly. The past family scandal means that he will have to ensure his chosen one is perfect in every way. It is vital that the family has all the appearance of respectability, class, grace and can fit in with the *ton*; otherwise, they will never recover their full place in society."

"Scandal?" Sophia asked. "Why do I not know of the scandal?"

"I have no idea about it either," Isabelle said.

"It happened a long time ago, when Sidney was barely out of leading strings, and has no reflection at all on the children." Mr. Carrington filled a glass of brandy and took a sip. "The earl's father was a bully. He made Mr. Daniels seem like a good, kind man. Wilberforce was incredibly cruel and selfish—I would even go as far as saying evil. I knew the family through their mother Katherine's father. Something happened after Sidney was born, which forced Katherine's family into action. One day they heard—how, I have no idea—that Katherine had been badly hurt, so they came here. Wilberforce was not expecting them, or they would never have gained entry, but they did and found Katherine beaten so badly that she was near death's door."

"Oh, my word! What about the children?" Isabelle asked, concerned for them all but desperate to know that Henry had not received a beating.

"They were unhurt. But when their grandfather, Alex, was trying to bundle them into his carriage, Wilberforce came forward and there was an almighty row."

"The poor things, they must have been terrified," Isabelle said.

"It gets worse," Mr. Carrington continued grimly. "Alex had no authority to take any of them away, but after a lot of argument, which came to blows at one point, Wilberforce allowed him to take Katherine, but insisted the children stay with him."

"Without their mother? At the mercy of a cruel man?" Sophia asked.

"Yes. It broke Alex's heart," Mr. Carrington said. "I do not think he ever got over the guilt of leaving them, especially as he was never allowed to see the children. That did not happen until after Wilberforce's death."

"Did their mother never return to them?" Isabelle asked.

"No. Alex had been afraid Wilberforce would find a way of hurting her because he never liked losing. Apparently, whenever he was drunk, he would rage that he would find her and kill her one day. Alex arranged for Katherine to disappear, after she had recovered from her injuries of course. No one in our circle has seen her since."

"And that is precisely why the earl will choose a wife carefully. Their name is not as respectable as it could be," Eliza said.

"Surely they are in touch with their mother now?" Isabelle ignored Eliza's comment.

"They do not know where she is. Alex took her location to his grave."

"Why, when their father died before he did?"

"I suspect that he thought she would ignore any communication from him. He once said to me that his actions had only given him his daughter for a short time, and that she would never forgive him for separating her from her children. She was in no fit state to have been left. I can understand why Alex did what he did, but I do not think he ever got over leaving the children behind."

"What a sad story!" Isabelle felt pity for the three children in such a difficult situation, but especially at the thought of a young Henry losing his mother.

"It certainly is. The family does tend to keep to themselves in a lot of respects," Mr. Carrington said but then chuckled. "Except for Sidney, of course. He has always been a neck-or-nothing boy, but he was too young to remember it all. Ruth and Henry were fully aware of what was happening, unfortunately. Alex said he used to wake up at night thinking he could hear the children crying."

"How awful! It does not sound as if there were any winners in such a sad situation," Isabelle said.

"All Alex could say was that he kept Katherine alive, but it came at a huge cost."

"I have always considered it a poor show that she did not return to the family home once she had recovered. No one should be allowed to abandon their husband and children, and if she had any sense, she would have come home to them," Eliza interrupted.

"And that is one of the reasons I consider you a silly young woman!" Mr. Carrington snapped. "I try to be patient with you, Eliza, but every time you open your mouth, you reinforce my opinion of you."

Eliza had gone puce, glaring at her grandfather. "I suppose you would rather me be more like her?" She pointed at Isabelle, as if disgusted at the thought.

"What have I got to do with anything?" Isabelle asked.

"All meek and mild, simpering at anyone who speaks to you when we all know Grandpapa's attention towards you is because of pity. Your mother repines that you are a freak, so I have no idea why he indulges you so."

Mr. Carrington jumped to his feet and grabbed Eliza's arm. "You have gone too far this time, you foolish chit."

Eliza struggled against the hold, but though he was in his dotage, his grip was strong. Flinging open the door, Mr. Carrington faltered upon seeing the butler, but kept hold of Eliza.

Showing no surprise at the sight in front of him, the butler bowed his head slightly. "His lordship requests the presence of Miss Carrington."

"He wants to see me?" Isabelle asked, still too affected by what Eliza had said to think straight.

"Yes, miss. He is questioning each person about the incident."

"Perhaps he thinks you capable of murder. It would not surprise any of us who know you," Eliza shot out before being dragged out of sight by Mr. Carrington, who was telling his granddaughter exactly what he thought of her and not caring who overheard him.

Isabelle stood and glanced at Sophia. "What a day!"

Chapter Eight

I SABELLE WAS TAKEN to the library, and once she was shown in, Henry stood to greet her. It was the type of room Isabelle could spend hours in, all the walls covered in filled bookshelves, a warming fire, though it was mild outside, and comfortable chairs placed in various locations within the room. Though she knew it was inevitable that everyone would be questioned, she was feeling a multitude of emotions as a result of what she had seen and heard throughout the day.

Henry had been seated behind a desk, which was stacked with papers. The wall sconce shed a golden light on his blond hair, and the shadows emphasised the width of his shoulders. Coming around the desk, he held out his hand, and when Isabelle put hers in his, he covered their hands with his other one. Hers felt delicate and precious within the comfort of his warm grip, a feeling she had never experienced before.

"Are you well, Miss Carrington? The shock must have been great indeed."

Isabelle was taken aback by the sincerity and concern in his words. "It is not something I wish to experience every day, but I am well, thank you." She hoped she would not regret her words when night fell and she was alone with her thoughts.

"Yet again, you are a revelation, Miss Carrington. You constantly surprise me. Please take a seat." Leading her to the chair in front of the desk, he only released her hand once she was seated.

"Thank you." Isabelle did not know how to respond to his comments. She was not sure if he was complimenting her or if he thought her a cold fish for not being affected as much as she should be.

"Please do not be alarmed at being unchaperoned with me. I am acting as magistrate in this instance, and I did not wish a maid to be present. I have a loyal staff, but gossip is inevitable."

"I am not alarmed." Isabelle was somehow unsurprised that she felt entirely comfortable despite being alone with Henry.

"I have been asking everyone in your group if they could go through everything that happened before and after Mr. Daniels's death. I am trying to put together a picture of events."

"And trying to find the murderer," Isabelle said.

"Yes, though I am not casting aspersions on your character."

"I do not see why not," Isabelle said. "As my cousin pointed out, I have been open with my dislike of Mr. Daniels."

Henry's lips twitched. "With relatives intent on putting you forward as a murder suspect, I would hope to find I was adopted."

"Oh, if only!" Isabelle smiled. "It would most certainly please my cousin and my mother."

"We clearly should have been allowed to choose our own relatives, for the ones we were given leave a lot to be desired."

"Your brother and sister seem perfectly normal. I often wished that I had siblings, purely for selfish reasons. If I had, my mother would not have so much time to focus on me."

"I would perhaps argue about Sidney being normal, but I take your point. Mothers can leave their mark, which is not easily dismissed."

Now knowing his history, Isabelle smiled in sympathy. He looked upset; it was clear he was still affected by what had happened. "But should we judge when we do not know their inner motivations?" she asked gently.

"I suppose not," Henry answered.

He was distracted, and though Isabelle was enjoying the

opportunity to speak to him so candidly, she knew they would have to move on to the reason she was there.

"Are you trying to lull me into a false sense of security, my lord? Earning my trust so that I confess all to you?"

Henry laughed. "I have not the talent to be so devious. I suppose we should get on with the task in hand, although it is nice to be able to relax for five minutes in all this madness."

"Will the house party end now?" For the first time, Isabelle was struck by the thought that when they left, it would be unlikely they would ever meet again. She had not known him beforehand, so there was no reason to think there would be any contact between them afterwards. She was so saddened by the idea that it almost took her breath away. Why had she let herself become so foolish over him? Was her mind wishing for the impossible? She had to try and concentrate on what Henry was saying, but she was struggling not to reveal some of what she was feeling.

"Not until the murder is solved, though that has not pleased some I have questioned."

"Does this mean they go to the top of the suspect list?" She tried to make her tone light, getting herself back under control when she knew they would not be leaving immediately. She was mortified by the thought that a man had been killed, and all she was concerned about was seeing Henry for a longer time. Her shallowness made her flush, but she could not help the longing she felt to be near him.

Smiling, Henry shook his head. "Now who is trying to shift the blame onto others? I see I am going to have to watch you closely. Now, let us begin."

The fizz of excitement at his words made Isabelle swallow before she spoke. She was being ridiculous, putting motivations where there were none. He had been very open about her not being his type, and she needed to remember that. She went through what had happened, relaying every detail.

"We were quite closely grouped, which was unusual, but I

think it was the excitement and thrill of being so near the balloon that caused the huddle."

"Who was next to Mr. Daniels?" Henry was writing everything down.

"Miss Ratcliffe was to one side of him, but given her reaction, I suppose she had nothing to do with it."

"Unless it was a clever ploy on her part."

Isabelle could not help a laugh escaping. "My lord, the poor woman was almost hysterical when she saw the blood on her pelisse. I hardly think she could have stabbed a man."

"Ah, see how easily she has you fooled." There was a twinkle in Henry's eyes before he became serious again. "You must think me an unfeeling brute to be funning with you. Please believe that I am taking this all very seriously."

"I know. I suppose an attempt at light-heartedness distracts us from the horror of the situation."

"Quite so. I am not suspecting Miss Ratcliffe in all truth. Until she started patting at herself, there was no blood on her gloves."

Isabelle frowned. "No, there was not."

"You seem troubled, Miss Carrington. Is there something amiss?"

"I feel I am missing something, but I cannot think what. I am sure it will come to me. To continue, I was standing to the rear of Mr. Daniels but slightly to the side. Mr. Corless was directly behind him, and Mrs. Fairclough was next to him."

"Who was in front of Mr. Daniels?"

"I am not completely sure who was at each corner of the square, if you could call it that, but I think it was Mr. Chesterton directly in front of him."

"Yes, that has been confirmed by some of the others."

"Then there was Mrs. Daniels to the other side of him. She was fussing over him as she usually did, and he was cursing her. Then she left to get him a drink of some sort. But then... Surely not!"

"What is it?" Henry leaned forward in his chair.

"When Mrs. Daniels left the group, she was holding her reticule in front of her in an odd way. And when she returned, she was no longer wearing gloves." Isabelle was frowning at the memory. It had seemed strange at the time, and that had been before they knew fully what was going on.

"Did she not leave her gloves on the table when she went to collect the drink?"

"I have no idea. I did not watch her once she had left us. She certainly did not return with them, and she was carrying nothing. There was no sign of a drink."

"I will check to see if she dropped anything on her way back," Henry said.

"Have you questioned her yet?"

"No, I thought to interview her last, as she is the main suspect."

"Now I know you are being obtuse. The way she fussed around him, no one could have been more attentive."

"Are you forgetting the appalling way he treated her? I think she, above anyone, had the most to gain by his death. She is a very rich woman now, young enough to marry again and certainly knowledgeable enough, through personal experience, to avoid another bully."

"But she is so…"

"Are you being too trusting again, Miss Carrington?"

"No! I do think the lack of gloves needs some explanation, but I cannot believe that she would have the wherewithal to plan such a thing. She has always struck me as someone who is very nervous, admittedly probably because of the treatment she received from her husband. But nevertheless, it would take a cool head to perform such an attack, especially in front of everyone. So many things could go wrong."

"Perhaps it was not planned? It could have been a spur-of-the-moment decision."

"I cannot believe she carried a knife around with her just in case she developed courage enough to stab him. And he was a strong brute of a man. She would have definitely come off in worse shape if she had tried to attack him. Surely it would have been easier to do it whilst he slept?"

"But then she could not have got away with it. They shared a room, at Mr. Daniels's insistence. There would be no one else to blame if he died overnight, whereas..."

"We were all gathered around, so it could have been any of us. No! I cannot believe it. You must be wrong."

"I hope I am, but the way things stand, she has a lot of questions to answer."

"Poor Mrs. Daniels. She will be devastated if she is innocent and knows she is under suspicion. I cannot help but pity her. She has not had a happy life with him."

"You have been very helpful. Thank you, Miss Carrington." His tone was soft, causing Isabelle to flush with pleasure, but she was soon brought back to reality with his next words. "I will send for Miss Belmont next."

"I feel terrible that I have pointed the finger at someone who has been treated so ill. If she did snap, no one would blame her; he was horrible towards her."

"He was, but he did not deserve to be murdered."

"I suppose not."

Henry stood and offered his hand to Isabelle, leading her to the door. "Do I need to put you back on the suspect list as you seem to condone his untimely demise?"

"I really hope you are funning, or I might just be offended." There was no sting in her words; his smile was enough of an indication that he was indeed teasing her.

"I have managed to offend you once when it was the last thing I wanted to do. I will never be foolish enough to risk that again." Lifting her hand to his lips, he maintained eye contact and let his lips linger. "You are a delight, and I would not have it said otherwise."

Stepping back from her, Henry opened the door and Isabelle walked out, confused, happy and intrigued.

Henry watched as Isabelle walked upstairs. He was being a damned fool. He could offer her nothing, but he wanted her like he had never wanted anyone in his life. Her lush curves just added to his need; he longed to feel those same curves in his hands while pulling her to him, longing to have her pressed against his chest.

Shaking his head when she went out of sight, he groaned. He had to find out what had happened to Mr. Daniels, and then everyone could go home, and he could forget her. Life would be as it had been, uncomplicated and although lonely, it was his destiny to be alone. Better a brother and uncle than a brute of a husband. He must never forget where he came from, nor whose blood pumped through his veins.

Henry had never thought himself an angry person, until after he had found the letter after his father's death. Then he had turned into a raging inferno of anger. Only when he had calmed enough to think straight once more did two things become apparent. The first was that he was never going to reveal what was in that letter. And the second was that his biggest fear had come to fruition—he did have the capacity to rage as his father had done. For him, that had been the day when he had given up hope that he was different than his father. But he would control his baser urges by being alone.

Chapter Nine

SOPHIA'S INTERVIEW WITH Henry did not take long, and afterwards Isabelle and Sophia decided to take a walk through the gardens. Soon, everyone would be preparing for the evening, and they both felt the need to escape for a little while.

"I expect it will be strained tonight. I do not envy Mrs. Parkinson as the hostess when half of her guests are suspected of murder," Isabelle said.

"I heard mutterings that some of the guests wish to leave."

"From what his lordship said, we are stuck here until they find out exactly what happened."

"He seems to have discussed quite a lot with you. It is clear that he values your opinion," Sophia said.

Isabelle shrugged. "I think I forced him into revealing more than he wished. I kept asking questions, which I am sure he only answered out of politeness. I am not presuming that he has told me everything."

"I do not think that is the only reason, but I shall save my breath because I know you will dismiss anything I say."

"He kissed my hand," Isabelle admitted.

Sophia immediately squealed at the words. "When?"

Laughing at her friend, Isabelle shook her head as if it was nothing, though it had meant much to her. "At the end of my interview. He walked me to the door and then kissed my hand.

He was so inconsistent throughout the whole of the interview. Half of the time, he seemed to have me on his list of suspects, and the other half, he seemed to wish to discuss aspects of what happened. I really do not know what to make of it."

"I do!" Sophia exclaimed. "He is clearly smitten with you. But to kiss you when you were in a room alone was very risky."

"It was my hand, and he is carrying out an investigation as magistrate."

"I would bet a quarter's allowance that he acted like that with you because he likes you as much as you like him. Oh, this is capital!"

"I am trying not to let myself get carried away and think too much of it."

"You might not, but I certainly will," Sophia said. "He likes you, just accept it and enjoy his admiration."

"But why would he…"

"Don't you dare say what I think you are about to utter, or we will have our first major disagreement. There is no reason for him not to like you, and I beg you think carefully before responding."

"You are a good friend," Isabelle said quietly.

"That I will agree with. Oh, look! Doesn't the site look sad now?" Sophia was looking at the hot air balloon. The basket had been secured, and there was a large net-like arrangement holding the balloon in place. Parts of the material billowed, as if straining against its tethers.

"It is such a shame that we did not get to see it in all its glory. I doubt anyone will be in the mood to try again."

"I suppose not," Sophia said.

Just then, they heard a shout behind them, and they turned back towards the house.

Sidney was running towards them, catching his breath for a moment before speaking. "Miss Carrington, my brother has requested your assistance most urgently and would be obliged if you would return to the house."

"Is something amiss?" she asked as they immediately started back to the house.

"Mrs. Daniels is being questioned, and Henry says he has never seen anything like it. She is hysterical. My sister tried to help, but Mrs. Daniels accused her of aiding Henry. He allowed me into the room, but she would not calm down even when I was there. Henry thought you might be able to assist."

"I am not sure what I could do, but I will try." Isabelle hurried, trying to keep up with Sidney's long strides.

"She says she can only trust you. You have shown her kindness and defended her," Sidney said. "I know I might come across as a fool, and I was beginning to detest Mr. Daniels, but I do not believe that she killed him. She has not got it in her."

Though Isabelle agreed with Sidney, she did not answer his statement. He had shown a preference towards Mrs. Daniels, and she was now a rich widow. Him being a second son would make her circumstances appealing to anyone without a large fortune of their own.

She had been musing that her mother would have reprimanded her for not caring that her cheeks were red from the heat and exertion of the hasty return if she had been present, but all frivolous thoughts disappeared when she entered the house. The wails emanating from the library sounded like an animal in pain, the cries only interrupted by intermittent words that seemed incoherent.

"Good luck," Sophia whispered.

"I think I am going to need it. Lead the way, Mr. Brook."

"I am under strict instructions to make myself scarce. She is convinced we are trying to trick her and working together to convict her. Please help her. She has been through enough at the hands of her husband," Sidney said seriously.

"I will do what I can to help, but I cannot make promises when I do not know who the culprit is."

"Then that is all I can ask. Thank you."

Isabelle walked into the library, feelings of guilt at the forefront of her emotions. She had told Henry about the gloves, putting Mrs. Daniels as the key suspect. She faltered when the faces of those seated inside turned towards her. Ruth looked upset and was trying to console a distressed Mrs. Daniels. Henry looked harassed, pained and quite clearly at a loss. When he looked at her, and his eyes flared with hope, she knew she would do anything she could to help him.

"Miss Carrington, thank goodness," Henry said.

At his words, Mrs. Daniels turned and sprang out of the chair and almost threw herself into Isabelle's arms. "Miss Carrington! Help me, please. They are trying to get me hanged! And I did not do it. I promise I did not do it!"

Isabelle held Mrs. Daniels while she sobbed, saying nothing but holding her tightly. She stood for a good ten minutes before the sobs finally started to subside. Choosing her moment carefully, she moved herself so she could see Mrs. Daniels's face. Silent tears were still making the woman's body shake, but she looked back at Isabelle.

"Come, you need to sit on this chair by the fire," Isabelle said gently, leading her away from the desk area. "I think a little brandy is in order." She shot a glance towards Henry.

"Mr. Daniels never let me drink anything other than lemonade. He said it was a waste for me to have anything else. I cannot believe he is not here. Is it some sort of mistake? I keep expecting him to walk through the door and curse me to the devil for being so foolish in believing that he has gone."

"No, I am afraid there is no mistake." Isabelle accepted the glass Henry handed her. "Here, take a sip. It will burn, but it will help with the shock and ease your nerves."

Mrs. Daniels did as she was bid, shuddering as she swallowed the brandy. "That is horrible."

"Is it? It is probably his lordship buying poor quality brandy." Isabelle did not react to the snort from Henry, her whole focus on Mrs. Daniels.

After taking a few more sips, she handed the glass back to

Isabelle. "Thank you. I do feel a little better, but I do not wish to have any more."

"What you have had should help calm you a little."

"I wish my parents were here. They would know what to do. They are good at sorting everything out."

"Have you answered his lordship's questions?"

"No, he thinks I killed Mr. Daniels, and I cannot prove that I did not!"

Speaking quickly before the tears started once more, Isabelle squeezed Mrs. Daniels's hands. "Surely you want to find out what happened to your husband?"

"Someone hurt him, and I don't know why. Who would want to harm him? He was the most generous of men."

Trying not to react in the negative or in surprise at the loyal words, Isabelle continued. "We all need to know what happened, and we do not know if anyone else is in danger."

"They could strike again?" The horror and fear in Mrs. Daniels's expression made Isabelle pause. She knew the young woman to be guileless, yet the situation was becoming more confusing the more she saw of her.

"We do not know, but it is possible. We need to find out exactly what happened to be sure."

"I do not know anything," Mrs. Daniels wailed, hurting Isabelle's ears.

"I promise that I do not wish any harm to come to you. I hated to see you hurt by Mr. Daniels."

"He did not mean it; it was just his way," Mrs. Daniels sniffed.

"Maybe so, but I did not like to see you so injured. It did not seem to me that you were anything but a doting wife. Do you believe me?"

"Yes, you were very kind to me."

"Thank you. I hope you believe me when I say I want a good outcome for you, but you need to be honest with us. Completely honest. Otherwise, if anything should be discovered later, it will not look good. Better to get everything out in the open now, don't you think?" Isabelle saw the look her words caused, and her heart sank. "Please be honest. I think you know more than you are saying."

"You will not believe me." Mrs. Daniels started to cry.

"It is worse keeping the secret. What happened to your gloves?"

The gasp confirmed that Mrs. Daniels was more involved than she was admitting to. "You saw them?" came the terrified whisper.

"Tell me what happened, and I will tell you what I saw," Isabelle said. She did not know how to question a potential murder suspect, but she was astute enough not to give Mrs. Daniels any information she knew.

It was a few moments before Mrs. Daniels spoke. Isabelle glanced at Henry when he started to move, but he stopped when Isabelle shook her head.

"I was doing my best to keep him happy," Mrs. Daniels finally said. "I was so excited to see a balloon at last that I didn't want there to be any reason Mr. Daniels would wish to return to the house."

"You were very attentive, more so than usual," Isabelle said.

"I knew he was annoyed with Mr. Brook and that it would not take much to cause him to lose his temper, but I was desperate to stay and watch."

"Go on," Isabelle encouraged her when she faltered.

"I must have been fussing too much because he slammed his cane several times, and I thought he must have hit his foot because he let out a grunt. I thought he would surely not stay if he had hurt himself and could not curse me as he would wish to." She took a steadying breath, but her tears started falling once more, this time silently. "I moved and touched his front, desperate to try and pacify him, but when I brought my hand back, there was blood on my glove."

"Why did you not raise the alarm?" Isabelle's tone was still very gentle; she was afraid of scaring Mrs. Daniels into silence once more.

"I do not know," Mrs. Daniels said, trying to wipe the tears, but as fast as she patted her wet cheeks, they were covered in fresh drops. "My first thought was that he would punish me so much because he had spilled something on himself. Then it sank in that it was blood, his blood, and I panicked. I needed to get away because the moment anyone saw me with blood on my gloves, they would think I hurt him, and Mr. Daniels would believe them and whip me. I could not stand the thought of another beating, not so soon after the last one."

"You did not know he was dead?"

"He was standing when I left! A dead person cannot stand, can they?"

"No, I do not think they can," Isabelle said.

"When I heard the commotion around Mr. Daniels, I threw my reticule and gloves into a flower bush and ran back. I thought he would be angry that he was injured somehow, but I could not believe he was dead. I don't know how it happened." Her sobs started in earnest, and Isabelle stood from where she had crouched beside Mrs. Daniels.

"I believe her," she said to Henry.

"I do too," Ruth said, looking in sympathy at Mrs. Daniels. "I will take her to her chamber and give her a little laudanum. I think she needs to rest. I did not appreciate quite what an innocent she is, the poor child." Ruth almost lifted Mrs. Daniels out of the chair, soothing her all the time.

Before they left the library, Henry stopped them. "Mrs. Daniels, please tell me where you hid your gloves. It is best if they are dealt with."

"It was under the rhododendron, the one I passed on the way back to the house."

Henry nodded, and Ruth led Mrs. Daniels out of the room. "Thank you, Miss Carrington. I am indebted to you."

"I am glad I could help. I feel so guilty for suspecting her now. Mrs. Parkinson is right, she is such an innocent. She is only five years younger than me, but I feel almost maternal towards her."

"Her explaining what happened does leave us with a problem."

Isabelle smiled. "Us?"

"You are very much a part of this investigation."

"Whether I like it or not, it would seem."

"Are you teasing me, Miss Carrington?"

"I would not have a clue how to even start."

"Oh, I do not know. I think you do it so naturally, it is even more endearing."

"I have not the wiles that the diamonds of the season employ. I doubt I could be bothered if I had the talent."

"Unfortunately for the diamonds, they are usually trained to such a degree that dancing with one is like dancing with any of them."

"Condemned with faint praise." Isabelle smiled. "Back to the point, though. I am presuming the problem we have is that we are back at the start."

"Yes." Henry rubbed his hand through his hair. "Who else surrounding Mr. Daniels had the motive to kill him?"

"Apart from me?" Isabelle laughed at Henry's eye roll. "You have got to keep me in mind."

"I refuse to do something so ridiculous, and I can do as I see fit because I am the magistrate. Do not laugh at me, Miss Carrington. I could easily arrange for a night in the assizes if you continue to insist you are a suspect."

"Fine. You have called me out. I am as much a suspect as you are," Isabelle said.

"Exactly. There is something we are missing in all this. Parts of what happened do not add up, and somehow the whole situation is not right. I am going to be staring at my bed canopy for the night if I cannot work it out."

The thought of him in bed did something inexplicable to Isabelle's insides, but she managed to pull herself together. "In that case, I will try to go over everything that I observed to see if I missed anything. Perhaps I have overlooked a snippet of information."

Henry walked her to the door and bowed. Isabelle hesitated but collecting herself, she left the room, disappointed that he had not kissed her hand like the last time. She then spent the next hour cursing that she had allowed her wishes and desires to run away with her. Of course, he did not like her in the way she liked him; she had been foolish to even consider it.

Chapter Ten

I T WAS NOT to be a pleasant evening for the guests. Mrs. Daniels was ensconced in her chamber, refusing to come out, whilst everyone else was surreptitiously regarding each other, each trying to work out who could be the murderer.

Ruth approached Isabelle when they were in the drawing room, an appeal in her expression. "I am sure it is the last thing you wish to do, but please, could I beseech you to perform for us this evening? I would suggest dancing, but it would likely turn into a brawl if someone uttered the wrong thing, given the current atmosphere. I need something that will soothe everyone's jangled nerves."

"The atmosphere is a little tense."

"It is! I had such high hopes for the party. Between us, I had hoped it would persuade Henry to hold more of them in the future, if this one went well. After what has happened, I am sure he will squirrel himself away once more as soon as we all leave."

Isabelle wondered why Ruth was revealing so much to someone who was a stranger to her a few days prior. Instead of nodding and politely changing the subject, she used the situation to her full advantage, as anyone smitten would do. She would scold herself later for being so calculating, but for now, she acted on impulse.

"You wish him to be out in society more?"

"Yes, he needs to meet someone who will understand him and be sympathetic to the effects of our upbringing. Hiding away, trying to dismiss his memories... It's not good for anyone, especially Henry."

And there it was, Isabelle's heart sank. She was to be the friend one could confide in, never the one considered as a possible partner. Taking a steadying breath, she cursed herself; having longings did not make them any more likely to occur. Henry was a handsome, single, titled man with a fortune. It did not matter that he had disparaged the debutantes; he could have his pick of society. Why would he consider her for even a moment?

"In that case, I will do anything I can to help. Just let me know when you wish me to perform."

"Thank you! I knew I could rely on you." Ruth squeezed her hands. "Your grandfather was right about you; you are a treasure."

"I would not go that far, but I like being useful if I can."

"Oh, you are so much more than that. We will let the gentlemen get settled, and then I will go to the piano."

When Ruth returned to her duties as hostess, Sophia approached Isabelle. "Have you had any more thoughts about who the murderer could be? I admit to being a little uneasy that whoever it is must still be amongst us."

"No, but it is so very sad," Isabelle said. "He wasn't a nice man, but he did not deserve such a brutal ending. I keep trying to remember something, but most of my attention was on what was happening with the balloon. How fickle does that sound now?"

"I was doing exactly the same; everyone was...except the murderer, of course. I just hope we find out who it is sooner rather than later."

As soon as the gentlemen joined the ladies, Isabelle approached her grandfather and smiled. "What mischief have you been spreading to Mrs. Parkinson?"

"I just pointed out that you were a delight and could be relied on in any circumstance. You are calm in any crisis, though I did not expect you to be quite so challenged before we came here."

Isabelle laughed. "You have described me to perfection." There was no bitterness in her tone; being useful to those around her was something she took pride in.

Ruth approached them and smiled at Isabelle. "Are you ready?"

"I am," Isabelle said and moved towards the piano.

Ruth sent a private smile to Mr. Carrington, and he winked in return. "You were perfectly right about them being perfect for each other," she said quietly.

"Glad to know you approve."

Ruth sat at the piano and Isabelle started to sing. Ruth had predicted correctly that their guests would appreciate hearing Isabelle once more. They might not take much notice of her during the day, but the moment she started to sing, everyone listened. Her face came alight with each note; she seemed taller, more confident and certainly very talented. Ruth had chosen a soothing song, and the sigh of relaxation was almost palpable around the room as everyone remained spellbound.

Eliza had remained silent when Ruth had spoken to Mr. Carrington, but at the smile on her grandfather's lips, she could not hold back. "You are wasting your time. The reality is evident for anyone who is not filled with foolish notions."

"Am I on a fool's errand?"

"Of course. I suppose it could be excused as the hopes of an aged relative, but be prepared for disappointment."

"Eliza, if you had half of Isabelle's qualities, you would be a hundred times nicer than you are. I despair of you, I really do. If this carries on, I will be forced to send you home."

"You would take Isabelle away from his lordship when you are clearly hoping she will make a match of it? You are doing it up too brown."

"Mind your language, young lady. I must correct you with regards to one point: I said I would send you away, but I mentioned nothing about anyone else leaving."

Eliza looked fit to burst but said nothing except a stiff *excuse me* and left the room. Sophia looked at Mr. Carrington when he sighed. He saw her frown and smiled.

"I thought I was doing the right thing, bringing Eliza. She can accuse me of being foolish towards Isabelle, but she fails to understand that I have been more foolish where she is concerned." Mr. Carrington looked at Isabelle as she sang, the room entranced by the beauty of her voice. "I hope more than anything that I can live to see her happily settled, for she deserves to have an escape from that mother of hers. What she suffers at the hand of the woman who should have her best interests at heart would test the patience of a saint."

"We appreciate her as she should be, but I know it does not make up for everything she has to withstand," Sophia said.

"She has good friends, and I value you just as much as she does."

"Thank you."

Henry had not meant to eavesdrop on the conversation, especially as they had been speaking in lowered voices, but after he overheard the spat with Eliza and Mr. Carrington, he could not help but be interested. That he had missed the words referring to him was a good thing, for he was struggling enough with his own feelings; he did not need to know that others were intent on encouraging a match between them.

What was it about Isabelle that drew him to her? He was still fighting against the pull he felt every time he was in her company. But when he heard Mr. Carrington suggest that Isabelle did not have a happy home life, it had felt like a punch to the gut.

He hated the thought that she had suffered, that she was still suffering. He could not understand why she would be treated so poorly. She was intelligent, pretty, funny and had the voice of an angel. How was she not appreciated by her family?

He remembered how much he had tried to be the perfect son, to not be the cause of a temper tantrum by his father, for that was what they were, though his father had been an adult and most certainly should have known better. Henry would do anything to try to keep the peace, to shield the others, to divert the man who was a violent bully. He eventually came to the conclusion that no matter what he had done, it had never been enough. The only aspect of it all that he had a modicum of control over was protecting Ruth and Sidney as much as he could. If that meant he took more than his fair share of punishments, he willingly did so. He was no martyr, just trying to protect those he loved.

It was with somewhat of a shock that the urge to protect Isabelle was as powerful, if not more so, than he had felt towards his siblings. Feeling an irresistible draw to her once more, he could not stop himself from approaching the pianoforte as they were looking to start a second song.

"I will sing the male part," Ruth was saying to Isabelle.

"There is no need. I will join Miss Carrington if that is acceptable?"

"Of-of course," Isabelle stuttered.

"Excellent. I hope I do not disgrace myself too much." Henry smiled, ignoring Sidney's pointed look and the curious stares of some of the guests.

Unaffected by the speculation, Henry concentrated on trying to give as good a performance as Isabelle's, though her talent far exceeded his. He couldn't resist turning to her as his deep baritone acted as counterpoint to her sweet tones, and their joint pleasure in the activity was written there in the sparkle of her eyes. When he caught himself longing to touch her lips, which were red and inviting, he averted his gaze and directed his thoughts to less foolish matters.

The duet finished to boisterous applause, causing Isabelle to flush.

"Thank you, Miss Carrington. Though I expect you have never had such a poor partner as me."

"Oh no, there have been far worse, I assure you."

Henry laughed. "That is praise indeed! I do not think I have ever had the pleasure of hearing such a talent. It is no wonder the ladies are reluctant to follow you." It was true—no one seemed keen to take Isabelle's place. "I think you have frightened everyone off."

"I do not see why," Isabelle said. "I cannot play as well as many, and to have more than one talent shows greater accomplishment than I can claim."

"Yours is a real gift, and no one having the pleasure of hearing you could think otherwise. I can feel Ruth's eyes boring into me. Could I beg for another solo from you? I think I have punished my guests enough."

Isabelle could not have refused a request so sincerely asked, but she most certainly could not have refused Henry anything.

"MRS. PARKINSON SEEMS to be determined to make the best of the unusual situation in keeping everyone occupied," Sophia said when the maid delivering a message about the party going on a walk had left the room.

"It is a sign of good breeding, surprising when you consider the upbringing she must have had," Eliza said. She was finishing off her hair to her own exacting standards, which many a maid had fallen short of and had suffered Eliza's caustic tongue as a result.

"We grow up despite our parents," Isabelle said.

"I suppose you are correct. We cannot choose our parents, just as they cannot choose us. I am sure many would change the hand they had been dealt with if they could, which in many cases is completely understandable."

Sophia stiffened at the pointed stare Eliza sent to Isabelle, but Isabelle shook her head ever so slightly at Sophia.

When Eliza accepted she was not going to get a response from Isabelle, she scowled. "I will go and see if Grandfather is ready to join us for the walk."

"I know, I know," Isabelle said the moment Eliza had left the room. "There is absolutely no point in responding, for it would turn into an argument, and she will never change her opinion. So, I refuse to waste the energy."

"You are far more patient than I," Sophia said.

"I cannot make such a claim, for she makes me seethe inside, but I know when to hold my counsel."

"You will have revenge enough when you become Lady Gosforth."

Isabelle could not help the laugh escaping. "Admitting to you that I am smitten with his lordship is not the same as him liking me."

"He singles you out far more than anyone else."

"We have had this conversation many times; I am the safe option. The one who would never be foolish enough to be carried away with ideas that might put him in a difficult position. Both he and his sister have commented on how much help I am, and there is no possibility of turning usefulness into affection no matter how much you try, or I would wish it."

"I hate it when you dismiss yourself so. Do not think for one moment that this conversation is over, but if we do not gather downstairs soon, Mrs. Parkinson will think we are not joining them. So, I will allow you this small reprieve."

A number of guests were already in the hallway. Isabelle had cursed her flushed cheeks the moment she noticed Henry. Thankfully, he was distracted by a conversation going on in the corner between Peter and one of the footmen.

"It was definitely here," Peter said as the footman showed one cane after another. "It is unique in that it has a silver tip on both ends and a longer handle; it has not got a round top like these others."

Sidney walked across the square hallway. "I told you to keep it in your room," he said to Peter.

"I did, and then I needed to speak to David a few days ago

and left it here for a moment."

"And you did not collect it afterwards?" The tone of Sidney's voice was drawing the attention of the others in the group. They were so unused to hearing him being serious, it piqued their curiosity.

"No, we became engrossed in the safety checks for the balloon ride. I must have left it here."

Peter's sudden pale complexion made Sidney almost growl at him. "Before the flight? You utter fool!"

"I did not do it on purpose. I just did not think!"

Henry intervened. "What is amiss?"

"We need to speak to you in private," Sidney said, now looking as sickened as Peter was.

"Follow me," Henry said, leading the way into his study and closing the door behind him when the two gentlemen had entered.

"I have a bad feeling about this," Isabelle said to Sophia.

"I agree, but what could it mean? Mr. Brook looked so angry, it must be serious."

"It must have something to do with what happened to Mr. Daniels. The way Mr. Brook reacted, he was clearly struck by something."

"This whole situation becomes even more confusing."

"I suppose we will find out in due course," Isabelle said as Ruth rounded up the walkers.

As they left the hallway to set out on the slightly delayed walk, a horse and rider arrived. When he called out to the butler that there was an express for Mr. Carrington, Isabelle and Sophia paused.

"I cannot imagine why an express for Grandfather would be sent here," Isabelle said. She moved towards the butler. "I will take the letter to my grandfather. It will enable me to find out why he and my cousin are not joining us on our walk."

Hurrying up the stairs, Isabelle could hear muffled voices coming from behind the study door. Whatever was being discussed sounded tense, as there were angry tones in the voices, though no words could be heard.

HENRY HAD RISEN from his chair, fists clenched, anger pulsing from him. "You are telling me that you left a weapon in my house, unattended and without anyone having knowledge of it or how it worked?"

"No one should have touched it!" Peter said, defending himself. "No man would take another's cane."

Sidney was seated in one of the winged-back chairs, his head in his hands. "But it was not picked up by one of us, was it? You said that Mr. Daniels demanded his wife collect his cane, and the top of his was similar to yours—I had already noticed that. He probably needed the support of the handle to help him move his bulk."

"She would have known which cane was his," Peter insisted.

"How many had silver handles like yours?" Henry demanded.

"Not many of them. I joked with one of the footmen that I did not envy his task in issuing the right cane to the correct owner, but at least mine stood out. I did not know that Mr. Daniels had a similar one," Peter answered.

"God dammit, Peter! Any one of us could have picked it by accident! The footmen could have been hurt, Mrs. Daniels, anyone!" Sidney snapped at his friend.

"Unless, of course, that was what you wanted to happen," Henry said.

Peter swung to face Henry. "What? No! I did not know that Mr. Daniels had one with an elongated handle. I genuinely thought that mine was the only one that had a silver base and longer top. It was all part of the mechanism. I am sure the bottom of it was unlike any other cane."

"The lower part cannot be seen unless it was taken out of the rack," Henry pointed out.

"Are you trying to say I contrived to get him killed?"

"You were very unhappy that he was no longer going to provide funds for you."

"That was because of Sidney's decision to abandon us. If I wanted to kill anyone, it would be your brother."

"He has not got a wife who inherits her husband's fortune on his death, and who has expressed an interest in ballooning."

"No! Surely you are jesting?"

"Do I look as if I am?" Henry asked.

Peter sagged into the nearest chair. "I did not plan anything, but I guessed what had happened when you did not have Mrs. Daniels carted off."

"What?" Sidney surged to his feet.

"I did not know for sure! I just suspected." Peter held his hands up as if to defend himself.

"Why the devil did you just create a scene with the footman in the hall if you knew what had gone on?" Henry was torn between incredulity and anger, and it was clear Sidney was barely containing his own fury.

"I said I suspected something, not that I knew for certain. I became wary when no one was accused of murdering him. And I knew how it would look if I came forward, so I pretended to have lost it," Peter said. "I never intended anyone to be hurt, I assure you. It was an oversight on my part, nothing more."

"And after you admit you deceived us all, you expect us to pat you on the head and send you on your way?" Sidney asked incredulously.

"No, well, perhaps, I suppose so," Peter said with a shrug.

"Did anyone else know about your cane?" Henry demanded.

"Sidney and David knew."

"As David was near the balloon, we can discount him, and Sidney was nowhere near the hall stand. Mrs. Daniels was the one to retrieve the cane. Had you ever shown it to her?"

"I don't think so," Peter said cagily.

"I think it is time you told the truth," Henry prompted him, showing a distinct lack of patience with the man.

"Yes, yes I did."

Henry shook his head in disgust. "I cannot believe Mrs. Daniels was our murderer after all. She is a fine actress to have us all believe her."

"She cannot have been!" Sidney exclaimed.

"What other explanation is there?"

"You might not believe me after my actions, but I do not think she did it," Peter said.

"What ludicrous tale are you going to concoct now?" Henry demanded.

"Before you condemn me, remember what happened," Peter snapped. "It was chaos in the hallway, and Mr. Daniels had taken the punches you were more than happy to issue," he said to Sidney. "Yet the man was still being obnoxious to his wife, and she ran to the canes and grabbed one. I would bet my own freedom that she had no idea which cane she had chosen. She would not have given it any thought, as we all know her efforts were simply to make the buffoon happy as quickly as possible."

"But then, how did the stabbing take place? You have shown me the mechanism, and it would be very hard to get it to work by accident." Sidney's tone was slightly less threatening as he considered Peter's suggestion.

"I have no idea," Peter answered. "I did not even notice my cane when we had secured the balloon."

"There was a lot of activity," Henry acknowledged. "Something is niggling at the back of my memory, so I am going to go over the notes I made during the interviews. How does the mechanism work?"

"It needs an unusually firm movement initially. It has to be a determined slam of the cane; otherwise, it would not be triggered in normal use. However, when it is set off, the blade shoots out with some force and immediately retracts."

"That sounds inefficient as a weapon," Henry said. "What if

you do not hit the ground with enough force? To me, there seems too much left to chance."

"Hang on, you showed me a mechanism, a safety catch," Sidney said.

Peter looked down. "Yes, there is one. It is to stop accidents from occurring. But if it was removed, there would not be the same need to be so rough with the banging motion. It is there if you are taken by surprise. But the safety mechanism could be removed for ease of use in certain situations."

"And this was not always on?" Henry was struggling to contain his temper.

"I am sure the safety was on. I think it was."

"I would question that you thought about any of it. Why would you bring a weapon to a house party?" Henry demanded.

"The balloon was once attacked by a competitor, so we needed some defence. It seemed the ideal weapon to keep with me without raising suspicion, and it could be carried with us without adding to the weight in the basket."

"And yet it was inside the house."

"I said I was distracted." Peter was becoming belligerent, and Henry concluded that they would get nothing further from him.

"I think you have told us enough for now. You might not have intended any harm, but potentially because of your carelessness, a man is dead, and someone else could have been arrested whilst you kept silent. It is a disgusting and unprincipled way to act in all regards," Henry said.

Peter went as if to speak and then seemed to think better of it. Head hanging, he left without meeting the eyes of Sidney or Henry.

The brothers looked at each other when they were alone, Sidney breaking the silence. "It might not be murder."

"No, but it is too early to be certain."

"We both know Mrs. Daniels to be incapable of such a calculating action," Sidney said.

"You take too much of an interest in her."

"As I have assured you previously, please do not concern

yourself or see something there which is not. I see a kindred spirit of a person in need of some kindness, that is all. I am not attracted to her in the slightest. I feel sorry for her, no more than that."

"You compare yourself to Mrs. Daniels?" There was no disguising the incredulity in Henry's voice as he moved behind his desk to sit down once more.

"Of course not! But we are both the victims of cruel actions, no matter how hard you tried to protect me." Sidney sent Henry a grateful look.

Henry had been pulling a sheaf of papers out of his desk, but at Sidney's words, he let them fall onto the leather inlay of the desk. "I hated being away at school, for I knew you would be his sole focus. I was glad when you were sent to school yourself. It meant I could relax a little through term time, at least."

"You should not have sacrificed yourself so often on my behalf. I still have nightmares about the beatings you took. You might have tried to hide most of it from us, but Ruth and I both know what we owe you," Sidney said, anguish in his eyes at the memory of the sounds they heard when Henry was being punished.

"There are no two people dearer to me than Ruth and yourself. You are my younger brother, Sidney, I will always try to protect you. The punishments did not last for long, especially as he got older." Henry tried for levity, but he saw Sidney's wince of pain. Sidney turned away, but Henry had seen the frown on his face. Waiting patiently, he was rewarded when Sidney spoke.

"I know I have cost you and Ruth so much anxiety about my actions over recent years, and I will always hate that. I do care for you both, even though... Oh, blast it! It does not matter!"

"Of course, it matters. If there is something bothering you, say it, and we can work it out together. There is little we cannot solve."

Sidney smiled wryly. "Sometimes, even you cannot put right the mistakes of the past, dear brother. Let us not dwell on things we cannot change but put our energy into proving that Mrs. Daniels is as innocent as she seems."

Chapter Eleven

ISABELLE ENTERED HER grandfather's bed chamber and found Eliza in deep discussion with him.

"It is polite to knock," Eliza snapped at her cousin.

"I am sorry, but there is an urgent express for Grandfather."

"There is?" Mr. Carrington immediately stood and reached out his hand for the letter. "This can only mean one thing. Isabelle, I need to speak to Mrs. Parkinson."

"Is there anything amiss?" Isabelle asked.

"I hope not," Mr. Carrington replied.

As Isabelle hurried downstairs to fetch Ruth, Henry came out of his study. "Miss Carrington, do you have a moment?"

"I am sorry, my lord, but my grandfather has asked me to seek out your sister as a matter of urgency."

"Ruth? She must be advanced on the walk by now. Giles, seek out Mrs. Parkinson and ask her to return to speak with Mr. Carrington at her earliest opportunity. I think she was headed towards the copse at the edge of the woodland."

"Yes, m'lud," the footman replied, immediately leaving the house.

"My apologies for seeming so heavy-handed, but it is of great importance that we speak."

"I do not mind. Now I know where they are headed, it is best I do not try to follow them."

"Do you dislike the woodland?" Henry was diverted from his task by the thought.

"Oh no!" Isabelle smiled. "It is very pretty, but my mother has always insisted that I do nothing to bring unbecoming redness to my cheeks. She continually reminds me that a true lady would never put herself in a situation where she might be forced to sweat. For young ladies are not to perspire but to glow prettily; anything else shows a distinct lack of breeding on the young woman's part and is a bad reflection on her family. You will not be surprised to find out that I am a sad disappointment."

They had arrived at the study by the time Isabelle had finished her speech, and Henry was laughing hard at her words.

"Miss Carrington, I am sure you are exaggerating. No one could have uttered those words in all seriousness. Even if she had, there is no need to worry. Your mother is not here, so you can trample all over my land with cheeks on fire, and I promise we will not think the less of you."

Isabelle loved his laugh, and that she had caused it made her even bolder. "I am, of course, being perfectly serious. It has often been my opinion that my cousin should have been my mother's daughter, as they have far more in common with each other than I have with my own mother. If I had been adopted, we could not have been more different."

"Yes, sometimes family can be a curse," Henry said. He grabbed the top sheet of paper and held it between them. "Especially where my brother is involved. When you described what had happened before Mr. Daniels's death, you mentioned him doing something with his cane. Could you explain again what happened, please?" Henry had been reluctant to change the subject but knew, for now, he would have to concentrate on getting to the bottom of the mystery, not enjoying Isabelle's company. Though that was what he was starting to long for, more and more.

They were interrupted by Sidney's arrival. Sidney nodded at Henry, and Isabelle saw the effect the action had. There was no longer any sign of joviality; instead, the frown he wore made deep grooves in his forehead. Isabelle had to resist touching him to try to ease his worry.

"Miss Carrington, please describe everything you can about what happened," Henry said, once more formal.

Isabelle went through the story, confirming that Mrs. Daniels had rushed to the canes and seemed to grab the nearest one to her. When she described the interactions on the field, Sidney stopped her.

"You are sure he hit the ground with the cane?"

"Yes, he did it several times with some force, a little unnecessary as he was standing on grass. It did not have the same impact as it would on a solid surface, but I think he did it to deter Mrs. Daniels's fussing."

"What happened next?" Sidney was more intense than Isabelle had ever seen him.

"He seemed to grunt, almost as if he was surprised, if that makes sense? It was a strange sound, and I suppose it could have been a warning to Mrs. Daniels. I have no idea. She certainly approached him when he made the noise, and then she left the group."

Sidney looked at Henry. "The fool effectively killed himself."

"I beg your pardon?" Isabelle asked in disbelief.

Sidney quickly told her about the modified cane having a blade which shot from the top of the longer handle. "I have just been to check Mr. Daniels's belongings brought in from the field, and it is amongst them. When he hit the ground with the cane, the safety catch was off, so he would have caused the blade to shoot out and retract. The final blow must have been the one that pierced him."

"Oh, my goodness! That is horrific!" Isabelle paled. "But surely someone would have noticed the blade?"

"I suppose with everyone clustered together, no one, including him, would have seen it."

Isabelle tried to recall the details of the scene. "He held that cane unnaturally close to his body. He leaned heavily on it."

"I think you have missed your calling, Miss Carrington," Henry said wryly. "Perhaps you should act as magistrate, not me."

"It must have gone up under his rib cage and pierced his heart," Sidney interjected. "What a way to die, by your own hands and because you were in a temper."

"He was not murdered," Isabelle said, sinking into a seat.

"You sound a little disappointed, Miss Carrington." Henry could not help the teasing tone in his voice or the fact that he wanted to tease her.

As he had hoped, his words caused the flicker of a smile. "Not at all. I am just relieved that we no longer need to look over our shoulders at every moment and be wary around everyone. It has been quite a strain for the whole party."

"You were never in danger. I had extra footmen in place overnight, one near your chamber."

"Thank you." Isabelle was surprised at the revelation but then remembered how fond they all were of her grandfather, which explained the extra consideration.

Sidney shot his brother an amused look before his shoulders slumped. "How the devil are we going to tell Mrs. Daniels. Beg pardon for my language, Miss Carrington."

"No need to beg pardon on my account."

"I can confirm Miss Carrington is the equal of either of us at cursing. I have had the privilege of hearing it myself," Henry said.

"We shall have words about revealing my foibles at a more appropriate time," Isabelle said, with an expression that made Henry look at her in mock innocence. "Could I suggest that I break the news to Mrs. Daniels? She is not going to take it well. I think we all do not wish a repeat of the scene earlier, when she was being questioned."

Henry grimaced and looked at Sidney. "I am ashamed to be relieved by Miss Carrington's offer. I am not good with crying women."

"You are not much better with any type of woman. Oh, listen to me being flippant when that poor woman is about to be told her husband effectively killed himself."

Isabelle had choked on a laugh at Sidney's first words but looked suitably remorseful at the thought of what the news was going to do to Mrs. Daniels.

"We can tell the other guests they are free to leave if they wish, and the funeral can go ahead without any further delay. I doubt many will wish to remain here just to attend the service," Henry said. "Many of the men actively avoided Mr. Daniels, and I cannot berate them for their reluctance."

"I will try and break the news to her as gently as I can. Perhaps she will be relieved that she can no longer be considered the murderer."

"Let us hope," Henry responded.

"I KILLED HIM! I killed my own husband!" Mrs. Daniels wailed for what felt like the hundredth time to Isabelle.

"You did not. It was an unfortunate accident," Isabelle soothed as she had been doing for some time since breaking the news.

"I was the one who gave him the cane! I thought it was his. I should have checked. Oh, my dear Mr. Daniels, I will never get over this! It should have been me!"

"Mrs. Daniels, you cannot utter such sentiments!" Isabelle was being gentle, but there was a firmness in her tone.

"How can I live with myself?" Mrs. Daniels continued to wail.

"Come, he would not wish you to be like this. It was an accident. No one could have foreseen what happened. No one is to blame."

"Everyone will think I did it on purpose. I know he shouted at me a lot, but it was just his way."

As there was still bruising where Mr. Daniels had struck his wife, Isabelle's thoughts somewhat disagreed with Mrs. Daniels's words, but now was not the time to try to convince the young woman that she had been given an unlooked-for reprieve from a life of cruelty.

"Would you like me to send a message to your parents?"

Wiping her tears, Mrs. Daniels frowned. "Why would I want you to do that?"

Hiding the surprise at the sudden change in tone, Isabelle tried to make her voice neutral. "I am sure they would want to support you through your grief."

"No! They would take over again. I will speak to David, Peter and Sidney, pay them what Mr. Daniels promised and then send a message to my solicitor. Mr. Daniels would not wish to have debts outstanding, and it would not be fair to his memory for me to withhold funds from the three gentlemen he thought so highly of."

"Quite." Isabelle struggled as to which was the more ludicrous—the change in Mrs. Daniels or the new version of her husband she was trying to create. "Is there anything you wish me to do?"

"No, thank you. I am grateful for your kindness, but I need to make arrangements for my future."

"Then I will leave you be. If you need anything, please do not hesitate to ask, and I will do my best to assist."

"I could not wish to have met a better person than you. You have been perfect. I thank you most sincerely."

As Isabelle left Mrs. Daniels's chamber, she mulled over the strange episode. The woman's actions and words did not add up somehow, but she reminded herself that she was young and probably did not know how to deal with the grief she was facing. The poor thing was probably going through a whole range of emotions.

Seeing Sophia leaving the library, she hurried downstairs to join her friend. "Would you like to accompany me on a walk?"

Isabelle asked. "I think the fresh air would be very welcome, and we never did get to join Mrs. Parkinson."

"Was being with Mrs. Daniels very testing?"

"Yes, complicated and confusing too, but enough of that. You are looking troubled, Sophia. Is something amiss?"

"I am fine, but you need to speak with your grandfather. He is well, but there have been revelations since you left to speak to Mrs. Daniels."

"What has happened now?" Isabelle let out a breath. "We thought we were coming away for a quiet house party."

"I have a feeling it has been the most eventful few days any of us have experienced," Sophia replied.

"I suppose I had better go and find out what else has been happening. At some point, I am determined to have that walk," Isabelle said, returning upstairs.

A few moments earlier...

MR. CARRINGTON HANDED Ruth the letter without saying a word. Seeming a little breathless because of hurrying back from her walk, Ruth scanned the letter before looking at Mr. Carrington, a multitude of emotions flitting across her face.

"She has been found," she said.

"Yes, and more importantly, she had already set out to return."

Ruth gripped Mr. Carrington's hand. "We are going to see her."

"Yes. Sooner than we all thought or expected."

"Thank you, thank you, thank you!"

"You are very welcome, my dear. I can only hope that your brothers feel the same way. I told you that it would be wise to let them know what we were doing in case of a result like this. They will have barely enough time to get used to the idea before she will arrive."

"I must tell them!" Ruth said. "Please excuse me. Oh, I cannot thank you enough."

"You already have." Mr. Carrington smiled at her. "I hope I have not prodded a wasp's nest with my meddling."

"I asked for your help," Ruth said. "I need my mother in my life. Henry does too. Only his self-imposed position as protector of the family has held him back from accepting how much he wishes to see her."

"And Sidney?" Mr. Carrington asked gently, regretting the flicker of pain his question caused.

"I hate to think that Sidney will be hurt in all of this, but only she can tell us the truth."

"True."

"We all deserve to know. And though it might prove a selfish action on my part, I want to see her."

"Wishing to know your mother could never be considered selfish."

"Let us hope not."

"YOU ASKED MR. Carrington to try and find her? Did you not believe that I was undertaking enquiries on all our behalves?" Henry asked, leaning on the mantelpiece, needing its support.

"Of course, I believed you, but Mr. Carrington knew people we did not. As well, you had a motivation not to find her, which I understand and do not blame you for."

Resting his head on the cool marble, Henry groaned. "What do you mean by that?"

"I know what Father told you," Ruth said gently.

"This could send Sidney completely off on a scheme of destruction." He closed his eyes, feeling dizzy. His life was starting to spin out of control.

"Henry," Ruth said, approaching and touching him gently on his shoulder. "You cannot take this burden on. You must let it go; it is not your responsibility and has never been."

"I am the head of the family. It is my job to look after you both," he muttered.

Ruth smiled tenderly at her brother. "You have cared too much and suffered as a result."

Henry moved away from her but met Ruth's sympathetic gaze. "I have not suffered."

"That is doing it up a little too brown, and we both know it! You were beaten more than Sidney and I put together, and it is something that has never rested easy with either of us. So do not try to convince me that you were fine."

"I could not have stood by and let you take the beatings. It did not matter to him who he was hurting, as long as he was hurting someone."

"The irony of all this is that you are afraid to let yourself become attached to anyone in case you turn out like him when you could not be more different."

"Thank you for saying that, but you have always been biased towards me."

"Of course, I have. You are my little brother. Just as you have felt protective towards Sidney. But perhaps you have tried a little too hard. One way or another, he needs to know about the reality of his background."

"You know about that?" Henry asked, finally standing straight. "For years, I thought I was the only one he told."

"I am a year older than you, and I also watched and listened," Ruth said. "I did not mention it earlier because I knew it upset you deeply."

"It will change everything."

"Will it? If it does, I think that could be a good thing. We are living in this half-life, not knowing the truth whilst society gossips at our expense."

"Are you bothered about that?" Henry asked in surprise.

"Yes, I am. I hate the fact that strangers could know more than we do or that they do not know what happened but are content to speculate."

"If they are talking about us, someone else is not being gossiped about."

"I am not sure that is correct," Ruth said with a slight smile. "When all comes to all, I am a mother who has muddled through. I want Mama to be a part of all of our lives, and I do not wish my boys to hear any gossip about us. If they do and ask for clarification, I want to be able to speak the truth. Secrets are not good for anyone."

"That I can understand." Henry's tone was gentle. "I just hope we do not live to regret it."

"Regret what?" Sidney asked, walking into the study without knocking.

"A five-year-old knows not to enter a room without knocking; it seems your manners leave a lot to be desired."

"Not in James's case," Ruth said of her eldest.

"He is clearly a young man who likes to know exactly what is going on, especially when the servants are aquiver with excitement."

"How do they find out these things?" Henry grumbled.

"The fact that you have to ask that, Henry, is a worry," Sidney said. "Now what is going on, and why do you both look decidedly uncomfortable?"

Henry and Ruth exchanged a glance, but Henry shrugged. "This is your news. You tell him."

"I will remember this lack of courage." Ruth raised her eyebrows at Henry. "Sidney, I asked Mr. Carrington to help in our search for Mother, and he has discovered her whereabouts."

"Oh," Sidney said, expression impassive.

"She was in France and travelled to the south to try and avoid Bonaparte," Ruth babbled. "She is already making her way home and has been for some time."

"Is this why you were pushing me for a decision about my

future? You want me out of the way before she arrives?"

Henry hated that the usually confident Sidney looked pale and vulnerable. He ached that he was letting his brother down by making him face something that, from his actions, Sidney had his own suspicions about. "There was no connection between the two things. In fact, I would suggest that you delay leaving."

"What is the point?" Sidney asked.

"I know you do not have memories of her, but surely you want to meet her after all this time?" Ruth asked.

"To have my illegitimacy confirmed? Yes, I know, Henry. Though to your credit, you have done all that you can to hide the fact from me."

"I had hoped that you did not know anything."

"I wish that I did not, but it has haunted me for years. I decided the best thing to do was ignore it as much as I could. I was happy... Well, perhaps happy is too strong a word, but I was content to remain in blissful ignorance." There was a note of bitterness in his voice, and it upset Ruth and Henry that their brother was suffering when they had both hoped he had been shielded.

"We do not know for sure," Henry said.

"Do we not? You were not present when Father would demand I get out of his sight. The by-blow he did not want. Every time he saw me, it just reminded him of what a gullible fool he had been."

"Of course, he wanted you!" Ruth responded hotly. "Or he would have let Mother take you when she left."

"According to his remembrance of events, she wanted you two but refused to take me. That told me all I needed to know."

"You have heard the words of an evil, vicious man," Henry said. "You cannot put any store in what he said. He hated the fact that she managed to escape him."

"He only wanted all three of us because he knew it was the thing that would hurt her the most," Ruth added.

"I appreciate that you would look forward to her coming

back into your lives, but forgive me when I do not show the same eagerness. The moment the house party breaks up, I will leave. If it meets with your approval, I will join the cavalry."

"Please do not rush into anything," Henry said.

Sidney laughed. "It was only a few days ago you gave me a time limit. For once, I am willingly doing as you bid, brother dear; enjoy the feeling while it lasts. Please excuse me."

He closed the door with more force than necessary, without giving Henry or Ruth a chance to say anything that might reassure him.

"I suppose he did not take it too badly," Ruth said with a grimace.

"I am not going to even attempt to answer that statement," Henry ground out. "I had better go and find him."

"Leave him be."

"No. I do not wish him to think that us acknowledging what Father said will change anything."

"It already has," Ruth said. "We are to have our mother back."

"Yes, and I hope to goodness that we all do not come to re-gret it."

Chapter Twelve

I SABELLE DECIDED TO escape from the chatter and speculation about what had happened and went for a walk in the grounds. She loved that the garden became less formal the deeper one ventured. She enjoyed formal gardens, but there was something freeing about being in a wilder, more natural space. Walking sedately until she had cleared the area where she could be seen from the house, she picked up the pace once she entered the woodland. As one so used to being watched and reprimanded about the way she should move, she breathed out a sigh, letting her bare hands scrape across the trunks of the trees, enjoying the roughness and undulating texture of something that was alive, but cared nothing of who she was.

Mulling over what had been an eventful day, she picked up a fallen twig and absentmindedly dragged it through the foliage which provided the ground cover. Her mind should have been on poor Mrs. Daniels, but all she could think about was that Henry had received some shocking news. She ached that he had seemed so troubled, as if he carried the world on his shoulders. And that had been before this latest news, which would add to it. She knew a troubled soul when she saw one, and she longed to be able to ease his pain in some way.

Yes, his words initially had offended her, but he had not said anything too awful; she had heard far worse. Her being not his type was hardly a surprise. However, he had been everything amenable and charming since, very much so. In fact, she had never felt so comfortable in someone's company as she did his. After that first blunder, he seemed to want to show her that he considered her someone whose opinion and help were of value. It was a new and novel experience.

She laughed quietly to herself. Since when did trying to find a murderer result in someone showing how charming they were? She was a strange creature to have enjoyed the time they had spent together discussing the case. And did she feel a sliver of regret that she no longer had an excuse to spend time with him? She almost snorted in disgust at herself, not noticing that she had inadvertently discovered the man himself seeking his own escape.

"Do my grounds amuse you, Miss Carrington?" Henry asked as he took a drag of his cigarillo, his eyes narrowing inscrutably as he blew a cloud of smoke into the air and leaned nonchalantly against a fallen tree trunk.

"You have a habit of startling me, sir," Isabelle answered, having jumped at his words, but her lips twitched in amusement.

"And what have I said to bring a sparkle to your eyes?"

A sparkle to her eyes? That almost sounded as if he was flirting with her?

Feeling tongue-tied, Isabelle blurted out the truth. "I was thinking what a strange house party this has been, though I do not mean it has been a bad one!"

Henry laughed and patted the tree trunk he was lounging elegantly against. "As this has indeed been a very odd time and has the potential of becoming more so, shall we break convention and enjoy a chat?"

Isabelle cocked her head, considering his words. "I suppose if you are willing to take the risk—for you would suffer more consequences than I if we were found—I do not see why not."

"I am risking more than you? What on earth can you mean by that when we are both fully aware it would be you who would be considered ruined if we were discovered here?"

Feeling bolder than she had ever been in her life before, Isabelle lifted her skirts, climbed over the undergrowth and perched on the edge of the trunk, keeping a little distance from Henry. She had not lost all sense of decorum.

"I have always thought it quite unfair that the stigma is always aimed in the woman's direction."

Henry smiled. He would ponder later how she always managed to make him smile and laugh, something only two other people could do. "Are you saying you are about to corrupt me, Miss Carrington?"

Isabelle snorted, making Henry chuckle. "I would not know where to begin."

"I cannot believe you are being coy and forcing me to compliment you further."

"Coy? That is one character trait that has never been linked to me before, although I like the thought of more compliments. As I have received very few, there can never be enough of those, in my opinion." Her words were said without pity or complaint.

"You could start by complimenting me. I believe that is how all compromising situations start." Henry was playing with fire. They should not be alone in such a remote place, but devil take it, he wanted to be with her, teasing and laughing. He wanted to act his age instead of feeling as if he had the world on his shoulders, so he pushed his sensibilities aside and was determined to enjoy being with the woman he could not stop thinking of.

Rolling her eyes, Isabelle did not try to hide her response; she was enjoying herself too much. "I am sure there is a queue of ladies just waiting for the opportunity to pander to your vanity. I do not expect you to be flattered by anything I might say. You will have heard it many times before and with far more eloquence than I could muster."

Stubbing the cigarillo out on the tree trunk, Henry blew out the last cloud of smoke. "I have noticed that you are very quick to put forth self-deprecating comments."

"I look for no sympathy or, worse still, pity when I say this, but the words hurt less if I say them first."

"Are you surrounded by obnoxious people? It certainly seems so from what you say. Mr. Carrington and Miss Belmont seem perfectly reasonable. Do they have a dark side that they are yet to show us?" The way Henry wiggled his eyebrows made Isabelle laugh.

"I am fortunate in my friends, but the wider populace is not very considerate when pointing out aspects of a person they do not approve of. Sometimes even family members can be as vociferous as strangers."

"Yes, being family does not make a person your champion."

"My mother would shudder at the thought."

"She must have known my father," Henry said dryly. "While I am fully aware of what a poor parent my father was, I am hoping the memories of my mother are not the construct of my imagination."

"You must be very torn." There was no point in pretending she did not know what he was referring to.

"Why?" The word was snapped out, and Isabelle jumped in surprise, causing Henry to soften his tone. In resignation, his whole body slumped. "I am sorry, Miss Carrington. I get angry when my brother's parentage is mentioned, but I was not referring to that. It is bad enough that society seems determined to keep the speculation alive."

"There is no value in my pretending I have not heard some of that, but I will say I only learned about it recently and from my cousin, who is one of the worse tattle-mongers one could have the misfortune to meet."

"Not your dearest relative then?"

"Not quite. However, if you were not referring to Sidney, I am confused about your meaning."

"I have memories, but I do not know if they are real or simply the longings of a child who was trying to make sense of losing his mother," Henry said aloud for the first time. "What if I have been wrong about her, and she is not the woman I—the three of us—

need?"

"As you have already said, you do not know what memories are fact or not. As she left you as children and is now returning to you all as adults, I am sure she will be as concerned about the meeting as you are."

"I suppose she could be uncertain. I had never thought of her being so."

"I would be terrified to meet three grown-up children. And from what you have mentioned about your father, I am sure she would have known he would not have been kind with her memory."

Henry's face twisted with derision. "He did everything he could to disparage her or ban us from talking about her. He even destroyed her portrait in front of Ruth and me. He took her image away from us."

"What a terrible thing to do!" Isabelle sat on her hands, or she was certain she would not be able to stop herself from reaching out to him.

"Wives do not leave husbands," Henry said.

"I beg pardon that I asked for details. I knew nothing of your family history before arriving here, and even then, I probably should have held my counsel. One thing Grandfather said was that your own grandparents genuinely believed that if they left your mother with your father, he would have eventually killed her. I do not think anyone—" she did not include Eliza's opinion in her words, "—would think it anything but reasonable for her to have left."

"No, but there are a lot of unreasonable people who are quick to make judgements."

"Their words might hurt, but do they matter really? If she comes back to you now and you all like each other, you have gained her in your lives for the rest of her days without the threat of your father hanging over you. I think society be damned!"

Henry barked out a laugh. "Thank you. You always seem to know exactly what to say."

His words sent Isabelle's stomach fluttering with warmth. "I sincerely hope it goes well and that she is the person you need her to be."

"I hope so too." Henry gazed at the trees, still troubled.

"Is that what brought you here seeking an escape?" Isabelle asked gently.

"That and the worry the gossip is true." Henry had uttered the words barely above a whisper.

This time, she could not help responding to him. Reaching out instinctively and touching his shoulder, Isabelle squeezed gently. "Whatever happens, he will always be your brother. Nothing can change that; your foundation is solid. It is clear he adores you and you him; that cannot be altered."

He put his hand over hers for the briefest of moments. "I hope you are right because I could not stand the thought of losing him."

"Anyone who sees you together can see the regard you have for each other."

"He is not very happy with Ruth or me at the moment."

"That will pass. He is probably as worried as you are that things will change."

"How do I convince him they will not?" Henry had turned towards her, desperation etched on his face. He needed to hear her words, for she spoke to him in ways that gave him hope.

"Speak to him, assure him and show him over time that your words are truthful. He will be hurt initially if your worst fears prove to be true, but if you are consistent, I am sure he will return to being the brother he has always been."

"Ruth said to leave him be, but I insisted on following him. I had not taken two steps out of the house before I was too much of a coward to see him and ran off into the woods."

"Mrs. Parkinson was probably correct. Give him a little time to accept what he is going to face, and when he is more himself, he might be receptive to what you have to say."

"You are right. He does need to mull the events over, just as we all do. Once more, thank you, and as much as I would wish to sit here all day with you, I think it is time we returned before they send out a search party for us."

"If we have to," Isabelle said with a reluctant groan.

Henry stood, and offered his hand, smiling when Isabelle placed her hand in his without hesitation, allowing him to pull her gently to her feet. "You make it very tempting to stay." Without dwelling on his actions, he pulled her towards him, and though she sucked in a surprised breath, she did not resist. "Miss Carrington, unless you tell me otherwise, I am going to kiss you."

Isabelle could not have stopped herself from leaning towards him, even if there had been a crowd of people around them. She was going to be kissed. By a handsome, charming man who was smiling down at her as if she was any other desirable young woman.

Sensing that this was her first kiss, Henry slowly lowered his head, and when his lips touched hers, she could not prevent a sigh from escaping. It was the sign Henry needed. Wrapping his arms around her, he deepened the kiss, teasing her and guiding her to respond to him. She followed his lead, and when he squeezed her behind, she was shocked and emboldened in equal measure.

"Wrap your arms around my neck," he whispered as he nibbled along her jawline.

Isabelle wasn't sure she had any command over her arms, but they clearly had a mind of their own as they snaked around his neck, finding his hair and grasping it, pulling him closer. The growl of pleasure was confirmation that she had done something right, and her heart soared.

Parting her lips willingly, she was explored and teased until all thought had left her and she was responding instinctively.

When Henry eventually pulled away from her, she moaned in protest, bringing a smile to his face.

Isabelle had never seen anyone as beautifully handsome in her life. His eyes were warm with feelings, cheeks flushed, and the sweetest, softest smile she had ever seen was on his lips.

"We must return, but believe me when I say I do not wish to," he said, kissing her with feather-like pecks.

"Thank you." It seemed to be the only thing she could think of to say. Nothing had prepared her for what was the appropriate conversation after experiencing the most delicious kisses.

Henry's smile grew wider. "You are more than welcome, but should it not be me who thanks you? You have been so much more than I expected. You are a gorgeous delight."

Isabelle had been touching his face as he spoke, but at his words, she stilled. "Please don't."

"I am sorry, I do not understand." Henry was still smiling, but there was puzzlement in his eyes.

"Don't utter falsehoods. Of all people, not you."

Now a frown replaced the smile. "What have I said that was wrong?"

"I know what I am. I would rather you not use words like gorgeous when we both know it to be untrue." Isabelle felt bereft when he stepped away from her.

"You have acted like this before, almost as if you are not worthy of being wanted. I do not understand why, especially after what we have just shared."

"I am being realistic." Her tone was defensive.

"I have just told you that you are a delight, one who I think is gorgeous, no less. How is that a bad thing?"

You mentioned being compromised, but we both know that in this case, it would be you who would be considered compromised unfairly."

"What? That is a ridiculous thing to say! Why are you being so nonsensical?"

Twenty-four years of being told that she was far from perfect, not as good as all the other girls filled her mind. Experiencing the best moments of her life, the perfect culmination of desiring him since almost the moment they had met, had resulted in all her insecurities overwhelming her and questioning his motivations.

"Look at me!" she finally said, hands indicating her curves. "I am the one who is laughed at for perspiring when dancing, who cannot remain fashionably pale because my cheeks become heated at the slightest thing. How can I take your words as anything but falsehoods when so many others are keen to tell me the truth whether I want to hear it or not?" She could not help the tears springing to her eyes, but she would be damned if she would cry in front of him.

"Do your friends agree with them?" he asked incredulously.

"Of course not. They are my friends; they would do anything to make me happy, including trying to convince me of things I know are not true."

"You believe the words of strangers instead of those of your friends? I cannot believe you to be so foolish."

"And there we have your real opinion."

Henry looked in complete confusion. "I have told you my true opinion of you. You are now looking for ways to find fault."

"I do not think so. I know what I am; it is you who is not being truthful."

Henry could not believe they were having this conversation after what they had shared. If it was not for the mortified expression on her face, he would genuinely think that she was funning with him in some way, though it was a poor joke. No, she truly thought he was uttering falsehoods.

At last, the emotion of the day caught up with him. He felt drained and exhausted and did what he had learned to do over the years to protect himself. He closed down.

"Then I suppose what just happened between us was a mistake on both our parts," he said stiffly, moving to pick up his hat.

His words felt like physical blows to Isabelle, but she raised her chin, stinging to know her suspicions had been proved right. He had kissed her as a spur-of-the-moment thing, not because he truly cared. If he had, he would not have uttered words he knew she would not believe.

"A foolish mistake which will never be repeated. Please excuse me, my lord." Turning on her heel, she stomped through the undergrowth until she reached the more flattened grass. Without looking back into the woodland, she returned to the house.

Henry had gone from melancholy and worry to amusement to passion in the space of half an hour. Staring blankly at the route Isabelle had taken, he eventually turned back to the fallen tree trunk and, slamming his hat down, he sat.

"What the bloody hell just happened?" he asked, bending forward and gripping his hair in both hands. The action made him groan as all he had done was remind himself of when Isabelle had curled her fingers in his hair, pulling him closer to her.

He had known full well that he had been looking for any opportunity to speak to her, to spend time with her, and today he had been unable to resist her when it was time to leave. His longing to touch her, to kiss her, had been too much to push to one side.

She might have never been kissed, but he most certainly had. And one thing was certain—he had never felt such joy when her innocent kisses had turned into something more passionate. Added to the mix, her luscious body and the instinctive way she reacted when he pushed her a little farther had nearly brought him to his knees with utter pleasure.

Then it had all gone wrong. He had never experienced such tumultuous feelings, and after the day he'd had, that was saying something.

Frowning over what she had hinted at from almost the first moment they met, he started to consider each comment she had made, for he could recall every conversation they had shared.

He began to accept how years of being verbally abused would affect a person. In some respects, his own family had suffered in a similar way, but there had been violence within that relationship too.

Sighing, he silently cursed himself. "I would not marry in case I turned out to be like my father, and she clearly feels worthless in a different way than I do. We are both afraid to trust someone who is not like everyone else." He did not care that anyone discovering him would think he was suffering from madness, talking to himself in the middle of the woodland; he had to mull everything over.

Eventually, snatching up his hat, he stood. "If there is one thing I am going to do, it is to convince that woman that she is indeed lovely. I just hope I can persuade her that those kisses most certainly should not be a one-off event. I do not think I could exist without more of them. A great deal more."

That decided, Henry walked out of the woodland with a new determination.

Chapter Thirteen

W HEN THE GENTLEMEN were left in the dining room, the ladies having withdrawn, Henry approached Mr. Carrington. "I need to beg pardon," he started. "I was unfair this afternoon. I have been looking for Mother, and the fact that Ruth had not told me about her approaching you made me react poorly. I was afraid of what finding Mother would unearth, without accepting that Ruth needed her just as much as any of us did."

"The bond between you is unbreakable, made partly from the experiences you have had, but she feels she needs Katherine even more now she is a mother herself."

"I had come to that conclusion myself," Henry said. "She has been surrounded by men; Father discouraged any of us from having friendships outside of each other, and she did not have the escape of going to school."

"He was probably afraid that if you saw not all families were cruel towards each other, you might start to fight back."

"I am not sure that we would have," Henry said. "We all tried not to escalate situations in our own ways."

"Yes, you were the good son, the protector. Sidney was the joker, charming everyone and Ruth, from what she has expressed in her letters, was and still is, the worried one, the quiet one."

"She is. I would also say she is the one who believes we will all find happiness, which is a real surprise. After what we experienced growing up, I would have expected her to be far more cynical, and it is to her credit that she is not."

"A matchmaker then."

Henry laughed. "Most certainly, but I have told her it is of no use." Why did he feel as if he was lying when he uttered the words? Pushing the thought aside, he tried to keep his expression bland but felt his cheeks warm at Mr. Carrington's assessing look.

"I can understand why you would wish that, but I find it very sad. There is nothing quite like having your perfect match by your side, easing the trials of everyday life. I hope one day you will find the person who will change your mind."

"You have been spending too much time in communication with Ruth."

Mr. Carrington smiled. "Not at all! I would not dare play matchmaker."

"Glad to hear it. One in my life is more than enough." What would Ruth think of the kisses he had shared with Isabelle? She would be over the moon to know he had liked someone enough to kiss them, not that he would be revealing the secret. The moment Ruth heard, she would be planning a wedding, and he and Isabelle would have no choice in the matter. Strangely, the thought of marriage did not scare him as it had in the past, and thinking of Isabelle brought a smile to his face.

"Is the house party drawing to a close now you have solved Mr. Daniels's death?"

"Yes. A few guests have mentioned leaving tomorrow morning. I think they are glad to be away, and I cannot blame them. I have a request of you, if you would not mind obliging me?"

"If I can help, I will."

"Would you and your party remain? I think it would help if you were here when Mother arrives."

"I can send the girls home; a servant to accompany them is all that is needed."

"No! No, they would be quite welcome to stay. It might help

to have a few friendly faces around the place."

Mr. Carrington smiled at Henry's outburst but did not offer any comment. What might have been an awkward silence was avoided when Sidney joined them. Once pleasantries had been exchanged, Mr. Carrington excused himself, leaving the brothers alone.

"What is happening with the balloon and its equipment?" Henry asked.

"Peter and David wish to try and fly it tomorrow if you have no objections. After that, it will either be sold or put into storage until they find another sponsor."

"Please stay," Henry begged, surprising them both with the appeal in his voice.

"What good would it do?" Sidney's usual joviality was gone. "We both know the truth."

Henry started to speak before suddenly clamping his mouth shut.

"Do not worry yourself. I know what is held within Father's papers; he told me about it often enough. The proof that I am illegitimate." Sidney's voice was low enough that it would not be overhead but not low enough to hide the anguish in it.

"There is a letter from Father, no other proof."

"Does there need to be more?"

"Yes! He was a beast of a man who would do anything to cause mayhem."

"I knew the moment you had found whatever documentation Father had left behind. But I presumed he had also told you earlier."

"How? I have not mentioned it to anyone else, not even Ruth."

"You changed towards me. You started to be almost nervous around me but yet more indulging, though to be fair, that part was pleasant enough."

The sad smile on his brother's lips was enough to take Henry's breath away. "I wanted you to know that it did not matter."

"You have always been a good brother, and I thank you for all your support, something I should have said before now, but it was easier to ignore the fact. Understand me when I say that I cannot stay and face her. The child in me still longs for a mother, and I do not wish for the tiny grain of hope to fly away the moment I meet her."

"If you stay for a few extra days, you could fly every day," Henry offered, and then rushed on. "And I will set you up to be a gentleman of leisure for the rest of your days."

Sidney smiled wryly. "I would be too expensive for you."

"Even if it ruins the estate, I will keep my promise."

"Why do you want me here so much, when it will only make things worse?"

"I do not think it will. In fact, I believe it will benefit us all. Yes, I believed the letter for a long time," Henry explained. "But when I discovered that friends of the family knew nothing of the situation, I could not help doubting its validity."

"It is hardly something that would be broadcast around."

"That is where I think you are wrong. She deserted him. And if he truly thought she had been unfaithful, he would have sullied her name to everyone he met."

"There was gossip about my birth, though," Sidney said.

"That you were his, and she was unwilling to acknowledge you. I have also heard that she had an affair," Henry said, hating being so open but knowing that it was needed.

"Whichever way it is, she is hardly likely to wish to have anything to do with me."

"The thing is, the stories were not repeated by him. He just claimed that you were illegitimate."

"From that, I am presuming the affair is the truth," Sidney said.

"This afternoon, I went to speak with the housekeeper," Henry said, once more knowing this could be a mistake.

"What did you want to speak to Mrs. Repton for?"

"About this."

"Wonderful. If the servants did not know about it, they will by now."

"I would not repeat the fact that you think she is a gossip, or she might throw out of the house herself." Henry was glad to see Sidney's lips turn up. "None of the staff were dismissed anywhere around the time of Mother's increasing or when she left. Nor did Father stop seeing any of his friends, as few as they were."

"I do not see that this helps," Sidney said.

"Of course, it does. There was no one for Mother to have an affair with. Mrs. Repton was adamant that Mother never went anywhere without Father; he would not allow it. She also said that though Father was a brute, Mother did love him and had to be forced to leave by her own father. She would have stayed."

"I do not want to raise my hopes, only to have them destroyed the moment she arrives."

"I understand that. But think—Father would have enjoyed telling us all the details if what he said had been true."

"Yes, he was that vindictive."

"Exactly! Which is why him not mentioning anything other than you were illegitimate is suspicious."

"I suppose so."

"We both need to know, but you especially need to hear the truth," Henry said gently.

"Because you need to find a real heir if it is true?"

"Most certainly not!" Henry said. "The letter will be destroyed once I have discussed the matter with Mother. No one will ever know the reality of what we feared."

"You are a good brother," Sidney sighed. "I do need to know. I suppose it is fear keeping me from facing her."

"I will be right beside you."

"Thank you. I will feel better with you there."

"Always." Henry decided enough had been said. They could do no more until their mother arrived, so he changed the subject. "I think we will be cursed to the devil if we delay joining the ladies any longer," he said, straightening his cuffs.

"Ruth is still trying to marry you off, you know." Sidney followed his brother's lead and returned to his usual teasing self.

"I know." Henry grimaced. "Unfortunately for Ruth, I have my own mind, no matter how much she tries to browbeat me."

"She will be displeased with you."

"I am sure I will be able to survive it."

"I like your confidence. I hope it is not misplaced."

Henry shot Sidney a look which was both derisive and a little disconcerted, making his brother laugh.

ISABELLE WAS UTTERLY confused. All she could think of, all she could feel, was Henry. Every part of her still tingled where he had touched her, and she had never expected kisses to affect her so much. She could not stop dwelling on the way she had responded and longed for those events to happen again. She had been ravished in the best possible way.

And then it had gone so horribly wrong.

Cheeks burning when thinking over how she had been, she wished she was more used to trusting the motives of others. Perhaps then she would not have reacted so poorly. She had barely been able to lift her eyes from her plate during the meal, and though ashamed that she had pushed the finest venison she had ever tasted around her plate, she could not face more than a morsel. It was a pity she had not been seated next to Mr. Sutcliffe, for she was sure he would have finished her food as well as his own.

"What is amiss?" Sophia asked when Eliza had gone to re-trieve her shawl and they had a moment to themselves.

"Nothing," Isabelle replied.

Tutting at her friend, Sophia pushed on. "I have never seen you so disengaged when in company. You have been distracted since you returned from your walk."

"I am just a little tired."

Sophia, hands on hips, glared at her friend. "If you wish ten years of friendship to end tonight, you are going the right way about it. Tell me to mind my own business by all means, but do not insult me by lying to me."

"Sorry," Isabelle said. "When I confess why I am out of sorts, you had better not betray it or bring attention to us."

"Go on."

"I kissed his lordship today. Many times."

Sophia squeaked, which she tried to turn into a cough. "Blast it. Eliza is returning," Sophia said as the door opened and Eliza entered the drawing room once more. "What happened? Tell me quickly!"

"We kissed. He said things, and I responded poorly. The end result was that I stormed off."

Isabelle could have laughed at the way Sophia's eyes had widened at her words, but she held her counsel as Eliza returned to them.

"I do hope you are not going to force yet another display on us as you have been doing, Isabelle. Some of the other young ladies have said that you are taking liberties by performing so often."

"I would have happily stepped aside at any point."

"When you are asked by the hostess, it is unbecoming not to promote your relation."

"Oh, do you think Grandfather wanted to sing?"

"You know full well that was not my meaning. You are insufferable at times. As your older cousin, I take priority."

"Of course, you do. If we were not leaving soon, I would make sure to always bow to your rank." Isabelle was nettled by her cousin's words. She wondered if Henry thought she had pushed herself forward to bring herself to his attention, and such damning thoughts increased her mortification.

"It is a sad affair that we are returning early. I do feel I was making progress with his lordship," Eliza said loftily.

Isabelle was at a loss as to what to say, so Sophia interjected. "In what way?"

"I have seen appreciation in his looks when he has glanced my way." Eliza was fixing her gloves and sitting up straight. "He clearly knows that I would be perfect for him. I can see myself enjoying being lady here. I think it will suit me."

"It is a substantial jump from his looking at you to marrying him," Sophia laughed, receiving a glare for her impertinence.

"When there is a shared connection, you just know. It is futile for either of us to fight it. I do wish we were staying longer."

"In that case, I have good news for you, child," Mr. Carrington said, coming up behind Eliza.

"Is the party not ending?" Isabelle's insides had started to squirm; with what emotion, she was not quite sure.

"It is," Mr. Carrington said. "Young Henry has some business he wishes me to help with. I said he could send you three home, but he is a congenial host and said you could stay."

"Are you sick of us already?" Isabelle teased.

"Of course, but that started even before we had arrived here." Mr. Carrington took any sting out of his words by kissing her on the cheek. "Do not look stricken, Isabelle. All will be well."

"I am a little surprised, nothing more."

"You are a good girl, a wonderful granddaughter, but an appalling liar."

This time, Sophia did not try to hide her laugh.

Chapter Fourteen

HENRY WATCHED AS his mother entered the room. She was here—the woman he had longed to see and had dreaded seeing in equal measure, mainly for what she could confirm or deny. He felt guilty on seeing the hope in Ruth's eyes as she watched their mother just as intently as he did. Of course, she was going to long for contact with her, even more than he did. Her musings had increased with the birth of each of her children; she had needed her mother, and he had not focused every resource he could on finding her. Ruth had always said he was a good brother, but seeing her expression now, he felt that he was indeed like his father and was ashamed at the thought.

He had memories of his mother, but a lot about her had faded in his mind, probably because as children, they did not dare to openly speak about her. If their father had heard, it was a sure route to receive a beating, and they could not trust the servants not to betray them, for they were in as much fear of their father as his children were.

He drank in her appearance, desperate in the hope that seeing her would help recall some of the memories he had forgotten. He remembered laughter, at least some of the time. How the child still within him longed to replace some of those darker memories with happier ones! He could only hope that she would be able to give him that, yet he was terrified of the upset her arrival could cause.

Her hair was woven with silver, and her skin was ruddy, not the fashionable pale preferred by the *ton*. She had the same eyes as he and Ruth had, which was surprisingly reassuring. As much as there had never been any suggestion that they were not her children, Henry would not have dismissed it as a final twist from their father's cruelty.

As Katherine looked at Ruth and himself, he could see her uncertainty, probably a mirror of what he was feeling. She wore a tentative smile, hopeful but at the same time fearful. It was clear she was uncertain of her welcome and hesitant about what to do next. He had to give her credit for being brave. He was not sure if he would have been as eager to face children he had been forced to leave behind, no matter the circumstances. They could hold nothing but ill-feeling towards her, and he gave her credit for visiting a house that would hold so many uncomfortable memories for her.

The silence in the room seemed to last for an uncomfortable amount of time before Ruth finally broke the impasse. "Mama?"

"Yes, my darling girl," Katherine said with eyes suddenly full of tears.

"Oh Mama! You are here at last!" With a sob of joy, Ruth cast herself into her mother's arms, no longer the restrained married woman but a young girl who had missed her mother so much, she always carried an ache around with her. And now her dreams had finally come true.

Neither woman held back their tears as they hugged, laughed and held each other again. No words were said beyond *Mama* and *my Ruth*, but it was enough for the moment to let out the emotions which had built up over too many years. Mr. Carrington and Henry looked at each other, at a loss for what to do, though not unmoved by the joy of the two women.

"You are so beautiful," Katherine said, eventually able to gather herself enough to speak a full sentence.

"I look like you, everyone says it," Ruth said.

"The letter said that you are a mother now. I can hardly believe it, but I am not surprised. You were such a caring little thing, looking after your brother every time he became upset. I thought you would be one who would have a large family."

"I have three boys who are all looking forward to meeting their grandmama, though I warn you they can be boisterous and mischievous too. They make me glad every single day, and I cannot wait for them to know you."

Katherine sniffed and had to wipe more tears away. "You wish me to be a part of their lives?"

"Of course! I have longed for you to come back to us, and I have always spoken to them about you. You have never been a secret. I have told them all that we shared when we were together."

"But I left you."

"From the little we know, you did not have much choice," Ruth said. "I cannot and do not blame you for what happened."

"You cannot know how much I appreciate you saying that, but it will be forever a regret of mine."

"I hope it will ease now you are back in our lives."

"I do believe that if I had stayed, one day he would have gone too far and killed me."

"He would have done," Mr. Carrington said gently.

"It took me a long time to understand that my family could not stand by and watch it happen, but it was years before I could admit that. I hated them for taking me away from you; it was the hardest thing I have ever had to do, and I had nightmares about it for years. You were always first on my mind in a morning, and the last thought before I closed my eyes at night and then I replayed my fears through my dreams. I am saying this not to gain sympathy; I do not deserve that. I just want you to know that I did not leave and forget about you. It was the worst thing I have ever had to endure."

Ruth shuddered. "I can only imagine."

"You have a good husband? Is he a kind man?"

"Oh yes." Ruth smiled. "He pretends to be a grump, but he indulges us far too much."

"There is no such thing as too much indulgence." Katherine smiled. "I cannot believe I am here, and you look so well, so beautiful. I worried so much that he would hurt you all, or worse, but I knew if I returned when he was alive, I would only make things worse for you. I could not stand the thought of hurting you all over again."

"We would not have gained anything, unlike now. I have been selfish, for I know Henry is eager to greet you too. He is just being a good brother in holding back." Ruth took her mother's hand and they approached Henry, who had remained in the background, but his eyes had barely left his mother.

"You have grown into a fine man. I am glad you have allowed me to be here," Katherine said, seeming to sense the hesitancy holding Henry back.

"You are welcome here and can stay as long as you wish. It is nice to see you again. I hope you are well."

"Henry!" Ruth exclaimed, but Katherine just smiled, not taking her eyes off her son.

"Would it be too much if I asked if you could indulge a mother's wish and allow me to embrace you? It is something I have longed for, but I will understand if you would rather not."

Henry moved stiffly towards her, and though he was far taller than his mother, he felt an almost boyish uncertainty when Katherine embraced him.

"Oh, my sweet boy." Katherine's voice cracked on her words as Henry pulled her closer.

"I dreamed of you so much," he said gruffly. Now that he was holding her, he clung to her as if afraid she would disappear if he let go.

"I am so sorry I was not able to return. I constantly came up with ideas of how to secrete you away from him, but as my family reminded me time and again, I had no rights to you, and the punishment would have seen us all hurt again. I had to hope that one day I would meet you, and you would be generous enough to forgive my actions."

"Father was a selfish brute. If either of us had been old enough to understand, we would have encouraged you to leave," Ruth said heatedly when mother and son finally parted.

"That is very sweet of you to say, but your cries and tears have haunted me every single day that I have been away."

"I am sorry you have continued to suffer," Ruth said. "Come, let us all sit down, we have a lot to catch up on." She was over-compensating for Henry's reticence, but in the excitement of her mother finally being with them, she correctly dismissed his hesitation as being overwhelmed by the situation and not that he was unhappy in any way.

For the first time since entering the room, Katherine frowned. "Where is Sidney?" she asked. "Is he well? Is he here?"

Brother and sister exchanged a look, but it was Henry who cleared his throat, always the one to take responsibility for the family. "Sidney is well, but he is a little reluctant to meet you."

"He cannot forgive my actions? I suppose it is no surprise when he will have no memories of me at all."

"It is not that," Henry said, looking decidedly uncomfortable. "I only found out recently, but it seems Father tormented Sidney with the reality of his birthright for many years. Father also told us individually and left me a letter to the fact."

"I do not understand." Katherine sent a look of appeal to Mr. Carrington. "Do you know anything about this? What could Wilberforce torment him with? Why would he put any doubt over Sidney's birth?"

"There have been suggestions and whispers over the years, I suspect spread by Wilberforce when he was in one of his moods," Mr. Carrington offered.

"According to Sidney, Father was very clear about Sidney being illegitimate, and as I've said, he wrote it in a letter for me to find after his death. But he had told me beforehand too," Henry said. "There was nothing we could do but believe it."

Gasping, Katherine covered her mouth with her hand. "That horrible, wicked man!"

"You will not get any argument from us on that score," Ruth said dryly.

"Why would he do such a cruel thing?"

"Because he could?" Henry said.

"Of course, Sidney is legitimate!" Katherine said hotly. "I did not dare to even look at another man, let alone dance with one! And as for anything more, I might not be the most intelligent of people, but I was not foolhardy. If I had done anything at all to cause jealousy or scandal, I would have received a beating. I was not in the habit of giving him any excuse to become angry or displeased with me, though very often he did not need one. If there had been any suspicion or doubt around Sidney's legitimacy, neither he nor I would be alive today."

"I knew it was not wishful thinking on my part when I could see Sidney's resemblance to Father," Ruth said.

"It does depend on the source of the gossip as to whether Wilberforce was the father and he had fathered a child with either a mistress or servant, and you refused to take the child on, or whether you had been unfaithful," Mr. Carrington said.

"I did not know you were aware of so much," Henry admitted. "I am coming to the conclusion that what I hoped was only known by a few was common knowledge amongst our acquaintances."

"These things tend to get around no matter how hard we try to control it, but I do try and keep a watchful eye on what is being said about those I care about, and would step in when I thought it necessary. It is sometimes a difficult balancing act not to cause even more speculation," Mr. Carrington explained.

"If Wilberforce had foisted someone else's child on me, I would still have accepted him," Katherine said. "It would have given me some leverage against Wilberforce's cruelty, and I would never have rejected a child who shared your blood. I know I am a stranger to you, and I am fully aware that you might choose not to believe me, but I assure you, Wilberforce is Sidney's father, and I am his mother. To add insult to injury, it was a difficult birth, and we were both lucky to survive."

"We need to send for Sidney," Ruth said, moving towards the bell pull.

"Wait! We should explain to him what we have been told first of all. He should be the one to decide if he would like to change his mind about meeting Mother." Henry had hardly finished the words when the door burst open. Sidney, looking stricken, filled the doorway.

"I need to know the truth, and I need to hear it from her."

Chapter Fifteen

"**W**HY DON'T YOU come in like a sensible human being and stop acting out some Cheltenham tragedy."

"It is easy for you to say," Sidney grumbled at Henry, but he entered the room and closed the door behind him. "I am sorry to burst in on your reunion, but I could stand it no longer. I need to know the truth, whatever it is."

Henry looked as if to speak, but Katherine interrupted him.

"I understand that Sidney needs proof, and that is completely fine. Let me try and think of something to convince him." Katherine thought for a while and then said, "The woman who tended me was a Mrs. Wheelton, who lived in the village. I have a bracelet, one of three that your father presented me with on the days after your birth. Each is engraved with your name and a thank you from him. I kept them as they were the nicest gestures he ever made, and I considered them a connection to the three of you. That is all I have in addition to my word."

"I know of Mrs. Wheelton," Ruth said. "She was not delivering babies by the time I was increasing, but I did speak to her once when I was visiting here and experiencing terrible sickness."

Katherine smiled. "Rest in the morning and ginger?"

"Yes! She also said you suffered a great deal with the early stages of your pregnancies." Ruth frowned, thinking back. "She said *all* of your pregnancies, which would suggest there were a few."

Katherine looked saddened. "There were some which did not go beyond those first weeks. I am not sure why, but it is the reason there is such a gap between Henry and Sidney. Mrs. Wheelton insisted on my staying in bed for most of my time when I discovered I was increasing again; she was determined that this time the baby was going to survive." Katherine smiled at Sidney. "Your father was not happy, but Mrs. Wheelton stood up to him a number of times. I suppose it was easier for her, since she had delivered him herself."

"Still a brave thing to do, her challenging him. He did not take kindly to anyone questioning his authority, whoever they were," Ruth said.

"I had to hide my laughter when, on one particularly difficult day, your father stormed in the room and demanded I get out of bed and play hostess to a group of friends he had invited round on one of his usual impetuous decisions. I always felt they were an excuse to cause a situation in which I would be at a disadvantage, not having prepared and then the consequences would be severe. Mrs. Wheelton stood, hands on hips and faced him as he cursed me to the devil for being a lazy good-for-nothing. She told him in no uncertain terms that she regretted smacking his bottom when he had been born to make him cry because he had not stopped whining since. If he could not be host in his own right to a group of men intent on playing cards and drinking brandy, then he could cancel the gathering and help her, especially as the chamber pot needed emptying and there was a danger that if she touched it, she would give in to her urge to pour it over his head."

"It is a miracle she was not cast out. He dismissed others for less," Ruth said, recalling many servants who had erred and were never been seen again, cast off without a reference.

"She dared him to try, when he turned puce and looked fit to burst. To add insult to injury, she threatened to put him over her knee if he took one step towards either of us. That was the point when he left and did not come to my chamber for two months."

"It sounds like Mrs. Wheelton was a force to be reckoned with," Henry said with the first signs of amusement since his mother had arrived.

"She was, but she was the most experienced nurse for miles. I do not think I would have delivered Sidney safely if it had not been for her."

Sidney had listened to the conversation in silence, which was in itself a rare occurrence.

Henry looked at him, always quick to respond to either of his sibling's discomfort. "What are you thinking?"

Sidney seemed deep in thought. "I do not know what to think. Forgive me," he said to Katherine. "I can believe that you are my mother and can confirm it with Mrs. Wheelton, but..."

"You are unsure if Wilberforce was your father," Katherine finished for him. "I only have the bracelet that he gave me, but you are old enough not to be put to the blush in understanding that affairs can occur, whatever I might say to try and convince you."

"I am sorry," Sidney said.

"There is no need to be discomfited." Katherine smiled at him. "I do understand. Your father has told you one thing, and I am claiming the opposite. You do not know me, and if our roles were reversed, I would have the same doubts."

"I want to believe you, and it is something Father would do to cause trouble, for I am sure he knew that if he were to die first, we would seek you out," Sidney said. "I just do not know what proof I will need to convince me of the truth."

"The only extra I can add is that surely you must have seen the resemblance between you and your father when you look at the portrait of Wilberforce and his brother Edward. They must have been around your age when it was commissioned. They are so alike they could have been twins, and you are so like them, more so than Henry or Ruth are."

"I do not know of such a portrait," Henry said.

"It was in the long gallery, next to the portraits of your

grandparents."

Henry shook his head. "No, there is a portrait of Father done some time ago, but I must have been around fifteen when he sat for it."

"I think I know the one you are referring to, Katherine," Mr. Carrington spoke up. He had been trying to keep to himself, only prepared to intervene when absolutely necessary. "I remember it from my first visit because your father fooled us all by saying they were twins. The joke lasted for days. I do not recall the detail of the portrait, only that it convinced us all."

"Why would he decide to get rid of it?" Henry mused.

"Probably to cause more mischief," Mr. Carrington said darkly.

Henry rang the bell pull, bringing the butler into the room. He explained about the portrait they were enquiring about.

"Why yes, m'lud," the butler replied. "It was replaced many years ago. The old master wished it to be destroyed."

"And was it?" Henry tried to ignore the gasp from his mother and Ruth; even his own stomach had tightened at the words.

The normally placid butler flushed a little and looked shamefaced. "The thing is, m'lud, I couldn't face throwing away such a fine portrait, especially with young Master Edward having died, so I had it removed to the back of the attics."

"You have just earned yourself a well-deserved pay rise, which will be doubled if you bring the portrait here within the next half hour," Henry said.

Turning on his heel and without another word, the butler left the room.

"I suppose we just wait now," Sidney said.

"In the meantime, we need to know more about you," Ruth said. "Let us get comfortable and you can tell us everything."

"There is little to tell." Katherine smiled, still looking unsure, as if she was afraid the situation would change and she would be asked to leave. She allowed herself to be led to a sofa by Ruth and willingly sat next to her daughter. The men accepted Ruth's suggestion and followed her lead.

"Did you have any more children? Where did you live? How did you support yourself? Have you been happy?"

"She occasionally takes a breath, but not very often," Henry said with an exasperated look at his sister.

Ruth shrugged. "I am curious."

"I do not mind the questions at all; it is a far better welcome than I was expecting," Katherine started, smiling at them all. Her gaze softened when it landed on Sidney. She might not have seen him since he was a babe in arms, but she was picking up the uncertainty rolling off him.

"I want to believe," he said, answering what he thought was an unspoken question from her.

"I know you do. Let me assuage your curiosity." She smiled at Ruth. "I could not stay in this country because there was the danger Wilberforce would find me, and even more of a risk was that I would weaken and try to see you three once I had recovered from my injuries."

"You would have done. It was your father's biggest worry," Mr. Carrington said gently.

"Yes, he knew me well enough to know that I would have tried to contact them the moment I was able. I was in too much of a raw state when I was first taken away to think the conse-quences through. It was decided that I would go abroad, but not anywhere around Paris or Bruges where I ran the risk of meeting someone I knew. We finally decided on the South of France; it was not one of the more popular locations that we chose, just a quiet little village."

"We?" Sidney asked, causing Katherine to smile.

"My sister, who was unmarried at the time, along with a maid and footman. I never betrayed Wilberforce before I left, nor did I afterwards. I took my marriage vows seriously and never wavered."

"After what he did to you, no one would blame you if you had. I only saw a few of the injuries, and usually after they had started to fade." Mr. Carrington sent a glare to Sidney. "They were far worse than what Mrs. Daniels has been subjected to."

Katherine flushed at the words. "It is in the past, and I have returned to my babies; there is nothing to gain by going over what went on then."

"They should know," Mr. Carrington insisted.

"They lived with Wilberforce for far longer than I did, so I am sure they are fully aware of what he could do. I am only ashamed that I left them alone to face it." Katherine's tone was sharp.

"I am sorry to add to your discomfort, but it cannot and should not be glossed over. He would have killed you," Mr. Carrington said.

"I know. He pushed me down the stairs once; I have no idea how I survived that. It was soon after you were born," she said to Sidney. "It was the incident that made me persuadable when my parents visited. I knew I would be no use to you dead, but when I agreed to go, I had not accepted that I would have to leave you all behind. I should have guessed, for there was no way Wilberforce would have just let me walk away with you three. His reputation would be sullied, and that was unacceptable."

"Did you find happiness in France?" Ruth asked.

"Bless you for asking. I have been content in my way, but there was never going to be another person in my life whom I would love. I was married to your father, and until he died, I kept my vows. When news reached us that he had gone, a long-time friend declared his feelings for me, knowing there would have been no point before then."

"Did you marry him?"

"I see you are a romantic." Katherine smiled at Ruth. "No, I did not. He could not understand that my heart always has been and forever will be tied to you three. He thought enough time had passed that I would be able to start again, but while you were not in my life, I could never start afresh. It was unfair to say that I would commit to him when, in reality, my heart was with you three, and no one could ever change that."

"Why did you not return when Father died?" Sidney asked.

"It was a combination of the difficulties on the Continent because of Napoleon and lack of funds to start on such a journey. I cannot claim poverty, but there was not a lot of money over the years. When my own father died, my sister and I only had a small allowance sent over to us; it was enough to live on but not enough for luxuries. I should have been more frugal over the years, but the moment I heard of your father's passing, I started to save and arrange for the journey. Even if you turned me away, I had to try. I stepped on English soil a few weeks ago and stayed with a friend of my father's. At that point, I am ashamed to say that I almost lost my nerve and decided that I could not approach you." She smiled tremulously as tears seemed to threaten. "Then my father's friend received Mr. Carrington's letter. I immediately knew that I had done the right thing in coming back, for you were open with regards to seeing me, even if nothing went beyond our first meeting. I consoled myself at that thought by telling myself that I would have seen you all, and that would have to be enough."

"That is why you were able to visit so soon. Oh, I am so glad you have come." The only reason Ruth did not throw herself at her mother for a second time was because of the knock on the door announcing the entrance of the butler. He was followed by two slightly dishevelled-looking footmen carrying a large, packaged portrait.

"That was very quick. We appreciate your retrieving it," Henry said.

"I had to know its exact location in case my decision was ever in danger of being revealed."

"Something we are now grateful for. You can leave it with us, we will unwrap it."

"Yes, m'lud."

Once the servants had retreated, Henry looked at Sidney. "Do you wish to have the privilege?"

"We both know you are asking that purely because you do

not wish to get your hands dirty," Sidney replied, a glimmer of his usual joviality on show.

"These cuffs are not kept pristine without care and consideration on my part."

"Buffoon," Sidney muttered, but he looked at Henry in gratitude before crouching in front of the package. Without ceremony, he pulled off the wrapping and stilled, an inscrutable expression on his face. Henry and Ruth rushed to his side when his knees hit the wooden floor with a dull thud.

Henry took a sharp intake of breath on seeing what had affected his brother, whilst Ruth started to smile.

"You are his son," Ruth whispered, her hand on her brother's shoulder.

"It could be your portrait," Henry said.

"It is as if I am looking in a looking glass and have two reflections gazing back at me. How can this be?"

"Because you are a Brook through and through," Katherine said quietly, wiping her eyes once more.

"I am?" Sidney seemed unable to believe what he was seeing, glancing between the portrait and his mother.

"You are, and I am your mother."

"Truly?"

"Yes. Truly, my baby boy."

"You are my mother."

"I am." Katherine choked out a laugh.

"I am not illegitimate. Not at all. Oh God! All this time, I felt as if I did not belong, felt like an interloper, and it was all caused through malice."

"Am I allowed to embrace you now, my sweet boy?" Katherine asked, leaving the sofa and crossing to where Sidney knelt.

Instead of standing as everyone expected, Sidney slumped further onto the floor and started to cry. Katherine moved to sit beside him and pulled him towards her, wrapping him in her arms.

"It is over now. We are all together. You are ours and always have been," Katherine soothed as wracking sobs shook her youngest child.

Henry looked at Ruth. "It has all been a lie." Neither had seen Sidney so upset, and it was tearing at their insides as the reality of what he must have suffered over the years sank in.

"It shows Father's level of cruelty and malevolence, made all the worse because it was towards his own children," Ruth replied, tears pouring down her face at the sight of her brother and their mother finally able to reunite.

"Everything was for naught. He played me like a fool. I should have known better, but I believed his lies. I should have questioned him more instead of being a Johnny Raw and swallowing all that he said."

"You were not. You were a good brother, trying to protect Sidney from the consequences of what you had been told." Ruth guessed some of what Henry was feeling, clearly upset that they had all been tortured by their father's actions.

"I need some fresh air," Henry said, moving to the door. "Please excuse me."

"Let me come with you," Ruth said.

"No, you are needed here," Henry said.

Ruth looked to follow Henry, but Mr. Carrington shook his head at her. "Let him be for now. This changes everything for him, just as it does for young Sidney. Give him time for it all to sink in."

"I do not want him to remonstrate with himself when he always did the best for Sidney and myself."

"He will for a time, and then he will accept that this revelation shows he is nothing like his father, which will eventually free him from his own demons which have been holding him back."

Sidney took a steadying breath as his sobs subsided. "And hopefully he will see sense and marry Miss Carrington," he said, standing and helping Katherine to her feet.

"Let us hope so," Mr. Carrington said.

"I feel I need to know all about this young woman if she is to become my daughter-in-law. I never expected there to be a wedding so soon after my arrival."

"Let us not get carried away with ourselves," Ruth cautioned. "You know full well Henry has said time and again that he will not marry."

"That was before Miss Carrington came into his life. He now follows her every move like a besotted puppy," Sidney said, his voice still thick with tears.

"You know he will roast you for a comment like that," Ruth said.

Sidney grinned. "He cannot harm me now. I am his full brother." His chest still heaved from his outburst, but at least he was smiling through his reddened face.

"You always were, to both of us."

"I know you accepted me, though none of us ever said anything, but I thought it was done out of pity or that you were just good people, trying to make up for my being a by-blow. Even though it was probably my own doing, I always felt like I was the outsider in the family, no matter what you did."

"Not helped by Father's machinations," Ruth said grimly.

Sidney took a deep breath. "I have let him spoil my life until now. I refuse to let it continue, but that does not mean I will not use it to my advantage, especially when I can get my own way with Henry." The teasing note in his voice had not fully returned, and they all knew he was still struggling with the morning's events, but there was a new lightness about him that had not been there before.

"Be careful, or he will send you into the regulars," Ruth warned.

Sidney grinned. "He would not have a legitimate member of the family in such a lowly regiment."

"I would not test him if I were you."

"Spoilsport." Sidney laughed. "It does him good to be tormented."

"I doubt he sees it that way," Ruth said with a shake of her head, relieved that the Sidney they knew and loved was still there.

Chapter Sixteen

ISABELLE FALTERED ON seeing Henry leaning against the balustrade. She took a step back in order to retreat before he saw her, but he turned towards her.

"I did not know you were out here, my lord. I did not mean to disturb you."

"You are not disturbing me. In fact, I am sick to death of being alone with my thoughts."

"I am sorry that you are troubled."

"Thank you. Most would think I am a fool. I have everything I could wish for, but I am still not happy."

Isabelle always felt she was a different person when she was near Henry, not restrained in the slightest, asking what should be left unsaid, especially in polite circles, so of course she blurted out the first thing that came into her head. "You are not happy at your mother's return? Forgive me, you do not need to answer that. I have no right to ask such an impertinent question."

Running his hand over his face, he sighed. "I am very happy she is here, but is it wrong of me to be resentful that I have lived the last years under an illusion? All the decisions I have made have been because of a falsehood, a lie told to cause the most hurt and uncertainty amongst the family. I have been on one restrictive path because of what I was told, and it was all for naught. I am sorry. You do not wish to hear my maudlin remonstrations, but I seem unable to stop myself confessing all when in your company."

Stepping closer and reaching out to him in an unconscious movement of comfort, Isabelle recollected herself in time, and her hand fell to her side without touching him. She hated that he seemed so upset and she could do nothing to help. All thoughts of what feelings his words had caused after they had kissed were forgotten the moment she saw him looking so lost. She could not help but respond to his pain.

"Does it not mean you are free to do as you wish now? You have no constraints; that must feel a relief?"

"It should be, and it is not a good reflection of my character that I am upset and annoyed at the change in circumstances, but it is what it is."

"Is there anything I can do to help?"

"Turn the clock back so that I stand up to Father and question him more, no matter what the cost, instead of being meek and not wishing to do anything to upset him. To stop myself from overindulging Sidney to the point I could have caused him to become a man with no redeeming qualities."

"Does it matter that you spoiled him? I do not know the particulars, but Mr. Brook is a very gregarious, pleasant young man."

"I suppose he is, but he has never accepted an ounce of responsibility. That isn't the worst of characteristics, I suppose. I expect I am more annoyed that I believed my father."

"Our parents are far from perfect, but they do tend to have an unfortunate amount of influence in our lives."

"That sounds like the voice of experience."

"Oh, it is, but I am—a big girl in every sense, so I will survive. Will what has happened cause problems for you all in the future?"

Henry had frowned at her words, but rather than speaking about what was causing it, he turned to look over the landscape. "It is not a good reflection on my character that I am bitter that my time spent trying to make Sidney live a respectable life was never actually needed. He is as legitimate as I am."

Isabelle did not waste time on reflecting that it was a great compliment that Henry was revealing so much to her; instead, she remained focused on him. "That is good news, is it not?

"The best of news. But when I should have been living the life of a rake and a scoundrel, I was the older, sensible brother who was looking out for Sidney all the time to try, in my bungled way, to make up for his illegitimacy. He has continued to live relatively wild. Now I find out it is because he expected to be cast off at any moment."

"That is sad to hear. It must have been an uncertain way for him to live, but would you really have been any different than you are now?"

"I do not understand your meaning."

"Your nature is to care about those around you. I am not so sure that you would have been the one to cause a stir across town. Your brother is far more suited to that role, even without his troubles hanging over his head."

Henry smiled despite his inner turmoil. "He most certainly is. Goodness knows what he will do now he is secure in the knowledge of his background."

"You might find he is more settled. Uncertainty may have caused him to act a little out of character, though I imagine he will always be one of the most popular gentlemen at whatever parties he attends."

"You seem inclined towards a sociable man."

Isabelle was taken aback by the comment. "I thought we were discussing your brother, not my likes and dislikes."

"I suppose I am trying to figure you out."

Isabelle laughed at his words. "I would imagine that task would take all of five minutes. There is nothing exciting about me."

"Isabelle! There you are! Grandfather sent me to look for you," Eliza said, glaring at her cousin.

"I am hardly hiding, standing on the terrace, in full view of the windows," Isabelle responded, but her cheeks had heated at the censure in Eliza's voice.

"If you were anyone else, you could be accused of trying to get his lordship into a situation most repugnant to him."

"Miss Hodge, I think I mistake your meaning. Please explain yourself." There was a steely coldness to Henry's tone.

"Do not worry, my lord. We are all looking out for your best interests, apart from my cousin, who always tries to gain advantage for herself. It is one of her less endearing traits and something you need to be aware of, for we cannot monitor her all the time."

"Eliza, come! Take me to Grandfather now! Please excuse us, my lord." Isabelle almost dragged her cousin away from the terrace and back into the house.

Shaking off Isabelle's grip when they were in the hallway, Eliza pushed Isabelle's shoulder. "You will not make a match with him. I do not know why you insist on following him around. It is pathetic. I have told you that it is me whom he looks at in appreciation, and yet you persist in making a fool of yourself."

"I am not following him around! I saw someone who looked upset and went to see if there was anything I could do to help."

Eliza snorted out a laugh. "As if you could offer him anything. You are deluded if you think otherwise."

"Why do you hate me so much?" Isabelle asked quietly, finally unable to take any more of Eliza's poison.

"That you even have to ask that question shows just how much you are wrapped up in your own little world."

"Eliza! For goodness sake, just come out with your grievances! I cannot spend time trying to guess your meaning."

"Everyone has always liked you. It might have been out of pity, but nevertheless, they all try to boost your confidence, your self-worth."

"Have you met my mother?" Isabelle asked drily, but Eliza either did not hear or chose to ignore the comment.

"Grandfather told me that I was going to be your companion

and that if you did not make a match of it here, I would have the pleasure of accompanying you abroad while we tried to find some sap who would have you. I was disgusted with you both that I was the one to be sacrificed because of you."

"I knew nothing of this," Isabelle said quietly.

"Grandfather said it was his wish to see you happily settled, and when I had helped you obtain a husband, I could go and live with your mother as her companion."

"Oh, Eliza. I truly did not know."

"He told me that as I get on so well with your mother, it made perfect sense, and she would leave you be if I was there to entertain her."

Isabelle had to acknowledge that her grandfather seemed to have her best interests at heart, but he was not being fair to Eliza. She could not believe that he would think Eliza would be happy with such an arrangement when she was always the one to say that she should marry before Isabelle as the older and, therefore, higher-ranking woman. As much as Isabelle loved her grandfather, he had erred on this occasion, and it seemed that instead of challenging him, Eliza had decided that Isabelle was the enemy.

"If he thinks I will sacrifice myself just so he can indulge you, he knows nothing of my character."

"Oh, Eliza, of course it is wrong of him. You are only a few years older than I, and you still have time to marry. I will speak with him."

"No! He swore me to secrecy. All he talks about when we are alone is how he needs to see you happy, how he will not rest until you are settled, even if it takes him the rest of his days. It is always about you! It is unfair!"

"It most certainly is," Isabelle agreed. "I will tell him I knew there was something amiss, and I forced it out of you." It would not be far from the truth, for Eliza had been consistently disagreeable towards Isabelle. But knowing the truth made her far more sympathetic to her cousin than she had been.

"As if he would believe that."

"That is a little unjust."

"According to Grandfather, everything to do with you is to be pitied and compensated for, when we all know the truth of the matter."

"And what is that?" Isabelle did not wish to hear the vitriol Eliza was spouting, even though she had probably heard it many times before. Still, it was inevitable the way Eliza had herself worked up. There would be no peace until Eliza had her say, no matter how Isabelle's stomach turned with the anticipation of the hurt the words were going to cause.

"He feels sorry for you," Eliza sneered, looking Isabelle up and down with derision. "Who could think anything else when it is your own laziness that has caused you to look so—so *grotesque*. If only you just did not eat as much, you at least would appear to better advantage. There would then only be your insinuating nature to go against you."

"Please excuse me, Eliza. I need some fresh air."

"But Grandfather wants to speak to you."

"I am sure you are more than capable of explaining my absence. You have such a way with words."

"But he will blame me for upsetting you."

Isabelle chose not to answer, for her voice would not have been steady, and she might utter words that she would later regret, no matter how deserved they were.

Walking as fast as she could, not caring whether her cheeks reddened with the exertion or she caused herself to overheat at the speed she moved, she let the tears fall as she left the house behind. Cursing herself, she muttered as she walked. She should be used to the accusations and insults. She was a fool to let Eliza's words upset her so, but with what had happened with Henry, she was feeling especially vulnerable.

Eventually, she reached the spot where she had exchanged kisses with Henry, the most wonderful kisses she would ever experience. She cursed herself further as she thought back to the pleasure she had felt being wrapped in his arms; it had felt like belonging for the first time in her life.

"Torture yourself, why don't you?" she muttered to herself.

Beyond the tree trunk, there was a mossy grassed area as soft as any carpet. Isabelle sank onto it, not caring that the pale peach of her dress could very well be ruined by her action. For the first time in a very long time, she let go of the emotions she normally held firmly in place, no longer pretending that the words and actions of others did not upset her. She could never let anyone see the real impact they had on her, but just for this moment, in the quiet space she had found, she released everything that had been swirling around, contained but struggling to get out.

How long she sat sobbing, she had no idea, but when her sobs had morphed into sniffs, she jumped violently with a squeak when a clean, white handkerchief seemed to appear in front of her face out of nowhere.

"I thought you might need this," Henry said gently.

Chapter Seventeen

Almost snatching the handkerchief from his hand, she covered her face with it. "You are very kind, but please go away. I am not a pretty crier and can only imagine the state I appear."

Henry chuckled. "You have mentioned that before, and I feel I am prepared for the shock."

"I wish I had the ability to make the tears cling to my lashes. Instead, they are all too eager to overflow onto my red and blotchy face." Isabelle was mortified that he was seeing her in such a way and had quickly scrubbed her face and blew her nose, knowing without doubt her skin would be full of deep red blotches.

Henry slid onto the ground to sit next to her. "I hate to see you so upset."

Isabelle could not help feeling comforted by his presence, no matter how ashamed she felt at that moment. "I am sorry to have taken your preferred spot. You clearly came to hide away and found a blubbering mess here instead."

"The only reason I am here is because I was still on the terrace and saw you head this way. I could see that you were distressed, and I could not stand by and do nothing. Am I being unfair to think your cousin caused it?"

"I am a silly wet goose. I have heard everything she said

many times before, but I think hearing that my grandfather pities me was just too much to bear. I had always thought he liked me for being me, which sounds ever so indulgent, so it serves me right to find out that he thinks I am a lost cause and is only acting because he feels if he does not, no one else will."

"He pities you? How the devil did she come to that foolish notion?"

Isabelle did not turn towards him but could not help smiling at his words. "She has had many conversations with him, apparently, about me and what will happen to Eliza in the future. I understand some of her annoyance. Grandfather is looking for me to wed, but has decided Eliza is to be a companion. If our roles were reversed, I am not sure I would be too happy about the situation."

Henry stiffened at Isabelle's words, but he steadied his voice, not revealing the surge of panic he had felt at hearing her grandfather's plans for her. "I take it he has someone in mind for you?"

"I have no idea. Eliza said he is looking for a poor sap who he can convince to marry me, but I feel even that will prove too much of a challenge for him, no matter how determined he is. I am sorry, I should return to the house." She attempted to get up, but Henry put out his hand to stop her.

"Please stay," he appealed. "I need to say that I do not like your cousin very much."

Isabelle grimaced at his words. "I should perhaps not mention this, but I think she has set her cap at you."

"She could have a hundred caps, and it would make no difference to my feelings on the matter. There is absolutely no chance ever that I would offer for your cousin."

Isabelle felt relief. There was a part of her that had expected him to be keen to discover more about Eliza when he knew that she favoured him. It did not matter that they had shared kisses; she could not believe he was interested enough not to be attracted to others.

"I have to ask you why you would think your grandfather pities you? All I have seen is adoration when he looks at you, and he speaks very highly of you."

"He does?"

Henry smiled. "Yes, he is always singing your praises."

"Oh, please do not think he would be planning on making a match between us!" Isabelle said quickly.

"Is a match between us so repulsive to you?" Henry tried to sound as if he was funning, but his tone was too serious to be disguised.

"It should be to you," Isabelle replied, looking at Henry for the first time since his arrival. Her heart lurched when she saw confusion in his expression. She had expected to see horror or even relief.

"Why? Did I not make myself clear when we kissed?"

"That was a moment of madness almost. There is no need to concern yourself about that; I know you meant nothing by it."

At her words, Henry stood and took a few steps away from Isabelle. Seeming to need something to do, he scuffed his boots against the nearest tree.

Isabelle watched him, unable to stop herself feeling sorry for his valet, who would need to restore the polish of the usually impeccable boots. When he turned to face her, she braced herself for a set-down. Hearing the words from family and strangers was one thing, but from a man she held in high esteem and thought about constantly, was completely different.

"Why are you so eager to think the worst of yourself? I have been puzzled by it since we met. I cannot understand why you would disparage yourself or allow others to insult you."

Isabelle felt her eyebrows raise at his words. "How can you ask me such questions when you can see me, what I am, how I am so different from others. I am mortified that you have touched my body enough to have no doubt how much it is flawed."

"Did you hate my touch so much?"

"Goodness, no!" Isabelle tried to recollect herself at her outburst, but for some reason, he did not understand her meaning. Drawing her knees up to her chin, she decided it was time to be open with him. "As I have been told many times, if I did not eat so much, I would be like every other young woman."

"What has your appetite got to do with anything?" Henry seemed genuinely befuddled.

Isabelle was exasperated. "Are you being purposely addlebrained?"

"Clearly, as I have no idea why what you eat is of importance to anything."

"Because I am fat!" Isabelle shouted at him.

Henry frowned at her. "You are beautiful."

Isabelle closed her eyes. "Please don't. As I said before, not you. I cannot stand falsehoods from you."

Taking a step towards her, Henry bent and gently took hold of her hands, pulling her to her feet. Seeing that she was wary of his actions, he did not try to pull her towards him, instead hoping his words would do the trick in convincing her of his regard. "Every moment I am awake, I am either thinking about the kisses that we shared, or I am trying to think of ways I can kiss you again."

"Why? Surely there are other, prettier, *slimmer* women you would prefer."

"I do not like the way you are keen to put yourself down when I see someone who has so many wonderful qualities. If I were required to list them, I would be speaking for at least an hour."

"Now you are being ridiculous."

"Fine. It would take two hours."

Isabelle did not try to hide the roll of her eyes or snort of disgust.

"Why do you think I asked your grandfather to delay your departure? I appreciated him being a friendly face when Mother arrived, certainly, but my main motivation was so I could spend more time with you."

"I am afraid of believing you." Isabelle's heart was soaring at his words, but she was more frightened than she had ever been. Scared to trust sentiments that went against everything she had been told before, she disbelieved that anyone could think of her as someone desirable. She wanted to, though. She ached to be the type of person Henry wanted, to be in his arms again.

"I have kissed few women in my life, and I have chased even fewer. With you, I am constantly at a loss as to what to do for the best when all I want to do is wrap you in my arms and protect you from those who do not appreciate you."

Taking a breath, and though she was sure that her face was still blotchy, her eyes red-rimmed, she smiled at him, feeling happier than she ever had. "You could always kiss me."

"And that is why you are perfect for me. You always say the right thing," Henry groaned, pulling her towards him, his lips touching hers. As he tugged at her hair, clips tumbled onto the grass, and her soft, blond tresses fell about her face. He needed to touch her, capture the feeling he had the first time they kissed. The sensation that he was with the one person destined for him. The person who completed him, filling every sense of longing he had ever experienced.

He loved how she responded to him, arms pulling him closer and her gentle moans and breathless gasps when he nibbled along her jawline and onto her neck. It made him feel like he could face anything the future held whilst easing the pain and troubles of the past. How she could do that to him simply by kissing him, he had no idea, and though he had been with other women, none had moved, soothed, or enticed him as she did.

"I want you," he whispered. "I need you."

Isabelle heard the words but did not register what they could mean. She was too consumed by his kisses to have any coherent thoughts. Every single nerve ending seemed to be reacting to him; it was an overload of feeling, and one she longed would never end. Responding to the way he gently guided her, she became emboldened, nibbling his lower lip and kissing his jawline as he had kissed hers. His groan of pleasure and the way he gripped her hair had her smiling as she trailed more featherlight kisses below his ear. She had never felt such pleasure and power intermingled, and she gained confidence, teasing him until he was breathing as heavily as she was.

"Isabelle!" The shout came from the direction of the house at the edge of the woodland.

Springing away from Henry, Isabelle glanced around her as if expecting her grandfather to burst through the trees at any moment.

"I will explain to him…" Henry started.

"No! Leave! Quickly!"

Isabelle pushed him in the opposite direction to where she could hear her grandfather's approach.

"But…" Henry started.

"I cannot disappoint him in this way." Isabelle winced at the look of hurt her words caused, but she could do nothing about it now. She would explain later, sure he would understand. Feeling relief and a huge amount of guilt when Henry turned his back and disappeared deeper into the woods, Isabelle was able to collapse onto the fallen trunk to try and catch her breath.

"Isabelle!"

"I am here!"

It was a few moments before her grandfather and Sophia came through the trees and into the opening. "Ah, there you are. We have been searching for you for at least half an hour. I thought you had abandoned us."

"No, I just needed some fresh air," Isabelle replied, scrunching Henry's handkerchief in her hand.

"I know what Eliza said. Well, the parts that I could get out of her. She should not have said what she did," her grandfather said.

"She should not, but I should be used to it by now. What she said about you pitying me hurt though."

"I do not pity you!"

"You can be honest."

"I am being! I adore you, you foolish girl. I am becoming tired that you always seem to believe the worst of what people say, never the good things that are said about you."

"Eliza is not the first to utter such things, and she will not be the last. Mother, especially, is very open with her opinions."

"I am glad that I can claim not to be a blood relation of hers. I only wish I could separate her from you."

Isabelle smiled. "You have done so much for me over the years; you have helped a great deal."

"And then I have made a huge blunder by bringing Eliza along with us. She is under no illusion as to how I view her actions. What is that grimace for?"

"She will dislike me even more if you have scolded her. She already thinks that I receive too much preferential treatment from you."

"If she had a fraction of the good qualities that you have, I would be able to put up with her, but she is a bad-tempered, ill-mannered termagant. This trip has proved that there are no redeeming qualities to her."

"You cannot say that! She is not so bad!"

"That is why I always want what is best for you. Your kindness knows no bounds, especially the many times when it has been tested to the limit."

"That is what we are always telling her," Sophia added, with a smile at Isabelle.

"I know what it is like to feel rejected. I would not wish anyone to suffer in the same way. I know the hurt and anguish it can cause, and I refuse to be part of an action which would inflict anything of the like on someone else," Isabelle said.

"Now you have put me to shame. I will try and find a solution that Eliza will be happy with."

"I think she just wants a husband. It is not an unreasonable wish on her part."

"That might be a difficult task to achieve, but remaining here now that Katherine has returned home is not going to find any of you a husband. I think we have done what we can to support the family and should make arrangements to leave tomorrow."

"Oh." Isabelle was overcome by a sense of panic. She would never see Henry again! He did not go out in society. "Do you think the family will go to town now their mother has been restored to them?" The question was said out of desperation, the only thing her anxious mind could think of.

"I doubt it. They have all expressed a desire to spend time getting to know her again without the gossips speculating and watching their every move. None of them needs that pressure, but especially Katherine, who is terrified she will make a mistake and be sent away."

"That makes sense, I suppose."

"Come." Mr. Carrington stood and held out his hand. "Let us go and plan our next adventure. I have an urge to see Switzerland, and you must join us, Sophia. The three of us can have a real adventure once we have found something to satisfy Eliza."

Isabelle took hold of his hand and let him tuck it into the crook of his arm. She was thankful there was no need for her to contribute to the conversation as they walked back to the house. Her thoughts were filled with the knowledge that she could have clung to the hope that Henry might follow her to town eventually, but there would be no chance of that if she was in a different country. That Sophia had noticed her reticence and would have questions for her later, she accepted as inevitable.

The problem was she had enough unanswered questions of her own.

Chapter Eighteen

I T WAS A small gathering that sat down to supper. Isabelle had expected the family to say they wanted a private meal but had been assured that they were all welcome. Isabelle was desperate to confirm that Henry was fine after the way they had parted but was seated too far away to enter into any conversation with him. He had barely looked in her direction, which was not a good sign, and she could only cling to the vain hope that it was the stress of being around his mother and not that her actions had upset him.

Even Mrs. Daniels had joined them, along with Peter and David. The only other guest to have remained at the house was Mr. Sutcliffe, and though he always smiled indulgently at Isabelle, she had never had to sit near him again. Instead, Eliza was seated next to him. Isabelle wondered if she would lecture Mr. Sutcliffe on his eating habits as she did Isabelle, but he seemed to be happy with her so far, so she guessed Eliza was being more circumspect.

"I think we should try flying the balloon tomorrow," Sidney suggested to Peter and David. "It can be one last goodbye."

"That would be a wonderful way to commemorate Mr. Daniels," Mrs. Daniels said, looking excited at the thought.

"Surely it would bring back too many painful memories?" Eliza asked, talking across the table.

Scowling, Mrs. Daniels straightened in her chair. "I think I am the one who would know what my husband would wish. He would not want me to miss an opportunity like this. He looked after my best interests."

As he had not shown any inclination towards her other than impatience, anger, and violence, her words were met with stunned silence.

Seeming not to be affected by the uncomfortable atmosphere, Mrs. Daniels continued smiling at Sidney. "I support your scheme just as my husband would have done."

"She seems to wish he be remembered as a saint," Sophia whispered to Isabelle, seated next to her because of the uneven numbers of ladies and gentlemen.

"I suppose it is easier to remember him that way," Isabelle whispered back.

"She seems very chirpy," Sophia responded. "At least she has recovered from her hysterics."

"I suppose her young age helps in that regard."

"She is young and rich, and I imagine it will not be long before she has remarried. Let us just hope her family does not force her into another mismatched alliance."

When the ladies had withdrawn, Ruth sought out Isabelle. "We will be sorry to see you leave tomorrow afternoon. It has been a pleasure to make your acquaintance."

"Thank you, that means a lot. I have enjoyed my time here, apart from what happened with Mr. Daniels, of course."

"Yes, he caused more problems than any of us could have imagined. Oh, listen to me! I am a heartless woman; the poor man is dead."

"He did not make it easy to like him."

"No, he did not. Miss Carrington, would you come to visit us at my home? I would really like to spend more time with you."

"That is very kind of you. Are you not intending to spend time with your mother?"

"I am, but she is going to visit with each of us separately to get to know us in turn. It is wonderful that she has returned to us, but her arrival has impacted us in different ways."

"But you are all glad she is here?" Fully aware that her concern was for Henry, Isabelle blushed at her words.

"Oh yes. I think her effect on my life is far simpler than it is for Sidney and Henry."

Isabelle was desperate to know more, but politeness kept her quiet. Fortunately, Ruth seemed happy to continue.

"Sidney is finding out for the first time about his history, knowing for certain that it *is* his history. With Henry, it is a little more complicated."

"How so?" Isabelle could not stop the words from being uttered. "Oh, I beg pardon, I should not have asked."

"Not at all. He swore he would never marry because he did not want to turn into Father, which he never would have done, of course. He has also spent years trying to protect Sidney and myself and given little thought to his own needs."

"It is to his credit as a brother and a man."

Looking pleased at Isabelle's words, Ruth smiled. "I am glad others, you, have noticed what a good man he is. I am hoping that, given time, he will make the right decision and be with the person who brings out the best in him."

"I, oh-I, yes, I think it is lovely to see how you all look out for each other." For a horrifying moment, Isabelle wondered if Ruth had somehow discovered that there was something between herself and Henry, and then she chided herself. Apart from the kisses, there was nothing to discover. Of course, she would want to see her brother settled with someone who would be good to him. Inviting Isabelle when Henry would be with his mother was not Ruth hoping for anything to develop between Isabelle and Henry; it was just a mark of friendship on Ruth's part.

"I think some time staying with me would be the perfect opportunity for us to get to know each other better without the drama of these last few days. I never thought I would wish for a quiet life, but after this adventure, I would appreciate some time to just have normal conversations that do not involve anyone dying or delving into a complicated family history."

"I can completely understand," Isabelle responded politely.

"Good. I hoped you would agree."

Sophia approached Isabelle after Ruth had returned to her mother's side, almost as if she was afraid to leave Katherine for very long. The two friends watched the family group for a moment or two, both of them touched by what they were seeing.

"What did Mrs. Parkinson want? You looked torn when speaking to her."

"She has invited me to stay with her at some point, though with Grandfather wishing to travel, I have no idea when that would be. She also hopes that now their mother has been returned and the family is more settled, his lordship will find someone to marry."

"She is matchmaking between you?" Sophia looked delighted at the thought.

"Not at all. She wishes to be my friend, nothing more, and I am not surprised at that."

"If you are about to utter some nonsense the way you usually do, I might have to box your ears."

"You can threaten what you like. I am not good enough for him."

"I certainly think he will be getting the best of the bargain, and if he does not, he is not worth the trouble."

"That is because you are a wonderful friend. It is a real pity we are leaving tomorrow. It feels as if once we go, I will find out this has all been a dream."

"I am sure it will work out."

"For once in my life, I am not going to disbelieve the words of others and say that I really hope that you are correct."

ISABELLE WAS ONE of the last to come down to breakfast. She had tossed and turned for most of the night, not wishing to leave

Henry but powerless to delay their departure. The family needed time alone, she understood that. She just wished she would not feel as if she was leaving her heart behind when it was time to board the carriage.

As she mulled over her thoughts, her attention was drawn to two footmen seemingly arguing in the hallway. Overhearing one of them say, *"You need to tell someone"*, her inquisitive nature was piqued.

"I could not help but overhear you. Is there something amiss? Do you need assistance?" Her voice was gentle, and her steady nature and lack of censure at such inappropriate activity for a servant invited confidences. Her smile was warm, and the two men instinctively turned to her, though they both towered over her.

"I am sorry, miss. We should not be so unprofessional." The lead footman glared at the other.

"If you have something you wish or need to seek counsel for, I am happy to offer my services without judgement, and as for professionalism, I find seeking assistance when appropriate is more a sign of ability than anything else."

The lead footman's shoulders sagged, whether it was in relief or defeat, Isabelle did not know, but at least they were going to seek her help. "If you would be good enough to come this way, miss."

Following them into the library, Isabelle could only wonder at what the problem could be.

"He will not tell the butler what he knows, for he fears he will be turned off," the younger footman started the moment the door closed.

"It must be something uncomfortable to speak of for you to think that." Wondering if she was about to find herself out of her depth, Isabelle waited patiently.

"It's the cane, miss."

"The cane?"

"Yes, the one that killed Mr. Daniels. Mr. Boyd handed it to me, saying that he did not need it anymore."

"Oh, I see." Isabelle pondered the footman's words. It was clear he thought that Peter's actions were odd. "Perhaps he did not wish to keep it after what happened?" she suggested.

"Tell her the rest," the younger footman urged.

Sighing in frustration, the more senior footman let out a huff. "I was there, in the hallway on the day Mr. Daniels died. When Mrs. Daniels ran to get his cane, I had already started to lift out Mr. Daniels's cane, but at my actions, Mrs. Daniels shook her head at me and grabbed the other one. I knew I had chosen the right one; there were only two that were similar."

"That is an odd thing for her to do. Did you tell his lordship any of this?"

"No, miss. I just thought she had made a mistake, thinking I was getting the wrong one, but when Mr. Boyd said what he did and looked pleased in a strange way, it made me feel right uncomfortable, it did."

"And now he's just seen Mrs. Daniels and Mr. Boyd go arm in arm towards the balloon," the younger footman added.

"I do not spy on guests, miss, I can assure you."

Isabelle could not help the twitch of her lips at his mortified expression. "If you did not notice things that were out of the ordinary, you would not be an efficient footman. Why would you think you would be cast off if you told anyone of this?"

"For accusing two of the guests of murder when it had already been decided it was an accident."

"Why did you think that Mr. Boyd offering his arm to Mrs. Daniels was unusual?"

"There was something about their manner, miss. If I had not known them before this morning, I would have said they were a couple in love, if you beg my pardon at being so blunt."

"I would rather you speak honestly about what you noticed."

"They were giggling and leaning into each other, all confiding like, and Mrs. Daniels was not upset in any way, like she has been since Mr. Daniels died."

As Isabelle was fully aware that all the servants, no matter how far away they worked from the main areas, could not have avoided hearing some of the hysterics Mrs. Daniels had gone through, she was not surprised at the words. As she, herself, had seen Mrs. Daniels's sudden changes in her manner, she believed what the footman was describing. What it meant would take more thought.

"Leave it with me," Isabelle said. "I will speak to his lordship about what you have revealed, and I assure you that you were perfectly right to tell me."

"I hope so, miss, because it won't half cause some trouble if I am wrong. Do you mind if we return to our duties, miss?"

"Not at all. Try not to worry," Isabelle said.

She remained in the library, thinking over what they had said and trying to remember every detail of that fateful day.

Everything had seemed confused, no one knowing what had gone on. She did not doubt the footman; servants usually knew far more than anyone else. Could Peter and Mrs. Daniels have planned such a complicated murder? There seemed to be so many things that could have gone wrong. She had no idea how a murderer's mind worked, but she did know that leaving so much to chance was not the best way to pre-plan so serious a crime.

There was a niggle that she could not shake off. Mrs. Daniels's actions were odd, and on more than one occasion she had been inconsistent, which only added weight to what the footmen had suggested, yet it seemed too fantastical. Deciding she needed to seek help to decide what to do next, she left the room, almost running into Sophia.

"Oh, I did not think you had risen yet," Sophia said. "I was just coming to wake you."

"I am later than I would have liked to be, but the footmen have just informed me about something I need to speak to his lordship about."

"Has Eliza risen yet?"

"Eliza? She was not in our chamber when I left. Has she not

been down to breakfast?"

"No. Your grandfather was despairing about the two of you, especially when Eliza had tried to persuade him to leave before the balloon flew this morning."

"Oh really? That does surprise me," Isabelle mused. "I wonder where she could be? I saw no sign of her clothes being packed, so she will have to hurry if she wants to leave so soon."

"Do you think your grandfather will leave early?" Sophia looked crestfallen at the thought of missing yet another balloon flight.

"I doubt it, especially with Eliza taking herself off somewhere. I wonder if she has had a change of heart and gone to see what is happening with the balloon? I will go and have a look for her."

It would also be the perfect opportunity for her to speak to, or at least observe Mrs. Daniels and try to gauge if the footman's suspicion was correct. That she should be seeking out Henry with the information she had been told, she pushed aside. He had so much going on with his mother that she did not want to burden him further. Let him enjoy some time with her. After all, none of the suspects were going anywhere. She would tell him later, but for now she would look for Eliza and observe how Mrs. Daniels and Peter were behaving.

"I suppose she could have gone into the gardens. I will look for her in the house just in case she has decided to stay indoors. I will join you in the breakfast room on your return," Sophia added.

"Good idea. I will not be long."

Chapter Nineteen

M RS. DANIELS WAS standing a little away from the activity
around the balloon, which Isabelle was grateful for. She
had not relished approaching Peter at the same time; he was far
more volatile if the arguments with Sidney and Mr. Daniels had
been anything to go by. She was no longer sure how a murderer
would behave and was beginning to question her actions when
Mrs. Daniels turned at her approach. It was too late to retreat
back to the house now.

"Have you seen my cousin?" Isabelle asked.

"No, was she coming here?" Mrs. Daniels answered.

"I have no idea, my grandfather was asking after her. I
thought I would check the gardens. Sophia is checking the
house."

"She has not been here while I have."

"It is not like Eliza to go wondering alone."

"I am sure she has not gone far. Who could, when we are
finally getting to see the balloon flight?"

"It all looks very complicated," Isabelle said, watching Peter,
David and Sidney work together.

"It is, but it will be worth it when it is flying," Mrs. Daniels
answered, her focus on the balloon site.

"Are you returning to your family when you leave? We are
leaving this afternoon ourselves. My grandfather is talking about

a trip abroad." She was trying to keep the conversation light, at least whilst she tried to work out if Mrs. Daniels had planned to hurt her husband. She had no idea what she was going to do if she came to the conclusion she had, but she had already realised that she had been very foolish for coming here alone.

"No. I am going home; there is much to sort out."

"I expect there is. Do you have someone who will help you? I cannot imagine it would be an easy thing to do alone."

"Peter will help," Mrs. Daniels responded.

"He is being a good friend to you."

"Yes, he is. Mr. Daniels was jealous of him, but I would not give up my friendship, no matter what he threatened or did. I do not abandon people who have my best interests at heart."

"He threatened you about having a friendship with another?" The fact that Mr. Daniels was suspicious of the so-called friendship could be dismissed, as he was so unreasonable, but it did add further support to the suspicions the footman had raised.

"Yes, he tried hitting me until I gave up Peter, but I was used to the beatings, so though I was bruised, it had no real effect."

"You should not have had to endure such ill treatment." Horrified at the accepting way the young woman dealt with her husband's utter cruelty, Isabelle's sympathy grew for her.

"Most of the time I know he was doing it for my own good, but when he threatened to lock me away because he thought I had been adulterous, it was too much. He said the asylum would take me because I had been unfaithful to him. I might have wished for a kinder husband, but I would never have betrayed Mr. Daniels."

"That was a horrible thing for him to threaten." Isabelle was struggling with the fact that if Mrs. Daniels did indeed murder her husband, she could not completely condemn her. She must have been in a terrible situation. But Isabelle remembered what the footman had said, and she collected herself. If the man had been correct, the murder had been pre-planned. That was not an immediate reaction to violence.

"I knew he was serious about it. If he did it, I would never be released."

"That must have been terrifying."

"It was. No one knew just how cruel he could be. Every single day since we married, he found some way to punish me."

"Did you not think to seek help from your family? Friends?"

"He would have simply laughed and called me a chit of a girl who reads too many romances. Then he would have dragged me back. I could not risk it."

"I suppose not, but now you are free."

There was a flash of anger on Mrs. Daniels's expression before she smiled and shrugged, seeming older than before, more calculating and worldly-wise. "I thought it would never end. But then he hurt himself and now for the first time in years, I know I will not be beaten." She sent Isabelle an intent look. "Am I wrong to be sad that he is gone, but relieved that he cannot hurt me anymore?"

Before Isabelle had time to respond, Sidney approached them. "I have been sent to gather everyone. Peter thinks it is time."

"Oh, good!" Mrs. Daniels clapped her hands gleefully, once more acting the young girl.

"I will return with you," Isabelle said to Sidney, now convinced that Mrs. Daniels had indeed killed her husband. She seemed to change too much. At one point, she was the hysterical widow, then turned into a woman making her husband to be some sort of kind benefactor, and now she was a wife who had survived a cruel marriage. Isabelle knew there had been violence, but she was no longer sure who the real Mrs. Daniels was.

"Oh, stay with me," Mrs. Daniels appealed. "I am too excited to be left alone. I want you to share every moment with me, just like Mr. Daniels would have done if he was still alive. God rest his soul."

"I need to find my cousin."

Mrs. Daniels took a firm grip of Isabelle's arm, pulling her in close. Isabelle wasn't certain, but there was something pressed into her ribs, and she had the horrifying thought that it was a pocket pistol. "I am sure Mr. Brook can send her to you if he should see her, wouldn't you, sir? Can you oblige us so that I can have Miss Carrington's company for a little longer?" she asked Sidney, all large smiles and guileless innocence.

"Of course, I will. Can't have anyone missing the main event. And you deserve to enjoy today after the suffering you have endured," Sidney said to Mrs. Daniels. "I will return soon, just like the Pied Piper, with everyone following."

Isabelle was torn but did not want to cause a scene by wrenching her arm away from Mrs. Daniels. After all, she could be wrong about the gun. But if she was not, Sidney could be hurt and she could not take that risk. Her self-doubt made her quiet when she should have been performing similar hysterics to those Mrs. Daniels was so good at. Instead, she remained stock-still while trying to send a look of appeal to Sidney, but he was too wrapped up in the day's events to notice. Her heart sank when Sidney moved away, completely oblivious to her discomfort.

All she could do was try to appeal to Mrs. Daniels's better side and convince her that she had not guessed the truth—that the woman had been involved in her husband's murder. "Well, I am sure I will still see the balloon flight from other parts of the garden. I should be searching for Eliza," Isabelle said, finally trying to pull away despite feeling the pistol in her side.

"You have not been interested in your cousin while you have been quizzing me," Mrs. Daniels said.

"I have been quizzing you? I had thought I had been offering sympathy and support," Isabelle said, trying to be guileless. "I am sorry if you think I have been intrusive."

"You really think I am stupid," Mrs. Daniels snapped.

"Not at all!" Isabelle said, fully aware that she was the one who had been foolish in the extreme.

"The death has already been dealt with, Miss Carrington. What reason would we have to go over something that was so conveniently declared an accident, no less?" Peter asked from behind Isabelle.

Swinging round, she cursed herself that she had been follow-ing Sidney's departure with so much concern that she had not noticed Peter's approach. Her situation became all the more alarming because of the manic, yet determined, look in his eyes.

"How do you think you will get away with killing me?" Isa-belle said, glancing at the knife now held ever so casually in Peter's hand. There would be little point in trying to escape as Mrs. Daniels had now taken her gun out of her pocket.

"You got a little over-enthusiastic and had such a terrible accident. Everyone will repine over the way you disregarded our advice, all because you were headstrong and wanted to have a trip in the balloon."

"Anyone who knows me would never believe I could act in a such a way," Isabelle scoffed, though her voice shook.

"Is this the same Miss Carrington who has taken the family by storm? Involving herself in every situation here, even becoming embroiled in a murder enquiry, though most young ladies would shudder at the thought. I believe your cousin would most definitely agree that though she was constantly reminding you about your inappropriate actions, you went ahead anyway. If that is not a clear sign of being headstrong, I do not know what is."

Isabelle could not argue about his character assessment, and her heart sank at the thought that everyone would believe she had involved herself in something she should have kept away from. "Your friend would hardly stand by whilst I was forced into the basket against my will," she said of David, who surely could not be involved. She was grasping at anything that could save her, or at least delay them enough until the others arrived.

"I am sure he would not, but then again, where is he?"

Isabelle's heart sank to see no one else on the field apart from the three of them.

Peter laughed at her expression. "When I received my dar-ling's signal that there was a problem, I saw to it to get rid of him. He is gathering farmhands to help us. A pity it will be too late to help you. Now come, there is no time to waste."

Isabelle was grabbed roughly, and though she struggled, Peter was far stronger than her and held her tight to him. Isabelle tried to wriggle and opened her mouth to scream, but when Mrs. Daniels held Peter's knife against her throat, she stilled.

"I do not want to leave an open wound on you, but I will if I have to. I am not prepared to let everything we have done be for nothing," she said in the same tinkling voice she usually spoke with.

Isabelle wondered how something that had sounded so sweet and innocent could suddenly sound so menacing.

"How did you know your plan would work? Too much of it seemed left to chance. Surely you risked it going wrong?" She wanted to know, but again was using her question as a delaying tactic.

"You want a big confession, do you? You wish me to explain every little detail to you, and then if this goes wrong, you can reveal all and be the heroine of the hour. I am sorry to disappoint you because you have always been very pleasant, but there is no time nor inclination for a baring of our souls. Climb on," Peter instructed. He hoisted Isabelle into the wicker basket, his rough handling making her tumble forward, landing on the floor of the basket on her hands and knees.

Turning around but remaining in her prone position, she looked at Mrs. Daniels, who was peering over the basket edge. "The balloon is not inflated. Someone will have returned before you are able to release it."

"Why would we do that? You might land safely. By releasing you now, you are more likely to be seriously injured and never recover."

Feeling a tug as something changed, making the basket lurch, Isabelle tried to cling on to the wicker with her fingers. "But what if my injuries are not too bad and I recover? I am strong and healthy, after all," Isabelle said, desperately playing for time.

"And as you are my dear friend who helped me so much

when I lost my beloved husband, it is only right that I help to nurse you to good health. If you develop a fever, or take too much laudanum, or even become delirious and throw yourself out of the window, no one will say anything other than I did my best. I will repine in a suitable fashion, of course."

It was not the only time Isabelle had felt helpless, but now, she felt sick to her stomach. Hearing condemnation and knowing there was nothing she could do about it was one thing, but this was terrifying.

"You said I had been perfect," she said to Mrs. Daniels. "I played into your hands, didn't I?"

"You were wonderful." Mrs. Daniels smiled. "I needed no one to think for one moment that I would be capable of murdering my husband, and Sidney and you were my defenders every step of the way."

"But then you were seen not taking the correct cane, though it was offered to you."

Mrs. Daniels scowled. "Blasted nosey beaks, the lot of you!"

"You are wasting time," Peter snapped.

"Do I not deserve an explanation?"

"No."

She should have taken the risk of creating a scene when Sidney had been there. Surely they would not have been able to overpower them both. Then she remembered the gun and realised that she could never have put Sidney in such danger. No, she had done the right thing to keep him out of the situation she now faced.

Every lurch of the basket was a rope being released, and though the balloon was only partially inflated, the way the basket was straining against the remaining tethers made her hope that the balloon would have enough air in it to become airborne. Being dragged across the ground in the basket was a sure way to a painful death, for she was certain to be thrown out of it. Every nerve in her body was telling her to scream, but she was frozen in fear, and any scream would be muffled by the snapping of the silk balloon as it flapped about in the wind and the distance she knew she was from any rescuers.

Mrs. Daniels squealed in what sounded like amusement and jumped away from the basket when Peter shouted to her, "Goodbye, my friend. This should be a valuable lesson to you; it is sometimes a bad thing to be too clever for your own good." Her laughter could be heard as she moved away from the balloon.

There seemed a slight pause, as if the balloon and basket were going to remain stationary, and then, with a sickening lurch, Isabelle was flung onto her side as the basket tipped and was dragged at an angle across the field.

Chapter Twenty

S IDNEY CAME FROM the direction of the morning room just as Henry was coming down the stairs. "Ah, there you are, it is time to join us outside," Sidney said. "I think even you will be impressed, and I, for one, cannot wait to finally be in the air. I have hurried everyone along."

There was movement behind Sidney as the others dispersed to retrieve their outerwear before making their way outside.

Henry rolled his eyes at his brother. "Even I will be impressed? I really am not the ogre you wish me to be."

Sidney smiled. "No, you are not. You are the best of brothers and always have been." He laughed at Henry's surprised expression. "Do not worry, I will return to my flippant self all too soon, but know that I mean what I say. You did everything you could to protect us, and I am aware that it came at a cost to you." He kept his voice low, not wishing for everyone to hear his sincere words; there had been enough speculation to last a lifetime, and he did not want to be faced with any more.

Henry smiled, relieved that Sidney was taking the meeting with his mother and all that had been revealed as a result in his stride. That he was not showing any signs of bitterness at being so ill-used by their father was a testament to his resilience and good nature. Henry certainly did not feel as congenial towards his parent.

"You have not turned out so bad yourself," he said.

"I am sure you are looking back with a sense of relief that I have now come to my senses and will become an upstanding citizen—after today, anyway."

"There is no doubt in my mind that you will always have a wild side to you." Henry grimaced. "Your blasted need for adventure has aged me before my time. I am sure I have wrinkles that would not have appeared for years if you had not been so hell-bent on living dangerously."

"I was just being a man about town, breaking hearts as I went along. I hurt no one as they all thought I was an interloper, and so never gave me a second thought. It was character-building for you; your life would have been far too sedate without me causing you issues." Both chose to ignore their trials with their father; neither wanted to spoil the new-found relief and contentment they were feeling. "Anyway, enough of this dilly-dallying, I promised to hurry everyone. Miss Carrington and Mrs. Daniels are already down there and have been eagerly waiting for everyone to join them."

At Sidney's words, a sharp intake of breath from the footman on duty caught their attention.

"Is there a problem?" Henry asked.

Turning pale, the footman stumbled over his words. "I-I don't know, my lord. Perhaps, probably not. Did Miss Carrington speak to you this morning?"

"No, why would she? Is there something amiss?" Henry was immediately alert and fully aware that he had not spoken to Isabelle since they had separated in the woods. His pride had been stung at the way she had wished him away from her, and so he had not sought her out at any point the previous evening. That he was always aware of her presence in the room had not helped his tumultuous feelings at their rushed separation.

"I did not think she would go straight to Mrs. Daniels, or I would never have said anything to her about it. She said she would speak to you."

"I have been with my mother this morning," Henry explained, trying not to show that his heart rate had increased at the footman's mortified, panicked expression.

"She is perfectly well," Sidney said. "They have Peter for company."

"Oh Lord!" the footman gasped. "My lord, we think Mrs. Daniels and Mr. Boyd killed Mr. Daniels, and I told Miss Carrington of my suspicions this morning."

"It was an accident," Sidney said, frown firmly in place. "What nonsense are you uttering, man?"

"I am sorry, sir," the footman choked out.

Henry rubbed his forehead. "What happened never felt quite right, but there was no proof to suggest anything other than an unfortunate accident. Are you sure about your suspicions? What caused you to think that murder had occurred? It is a very serious thing you are saying."

The footman quickly repeated what he had told Isabelle. "I am sorry I did not come immediately to you, my lord. I was afraid I would be cast off for making accusations against one of your guests. It was only that Miss Carrington overheard me discussing it with Benson, and she insisted it was important to tell her. She was very nice about it and promised she would speak to you. I never for one moment thought she would approach either Mrs. Daniels or Mr. Boyd, or I would not have said a word."

"Of course, she insisted on knowing what was happening. She was not completely happy with the outcome of our investigations either. It seemed like there was something we had missed, and now we know that our distrust was well-founded. Why on earth would she decide to take matters into her own hands? For goodness sake, if you are right, she has gone to speak to the murderers. Alone," Henry ground out. "Tell everyone that we will meet them at the field," he instructed the footman. "Sidney, we need to go and check on them without waiting for everyone else. I have a really bad feeling about this. If they know she suspects foul play, I do not think either will take kindly to it."

There was no joviality visible on Sidney's part; he just followed his brother in silence as they hurried out of the house. The footman faltered only for a moment before running to get the assistance of his fellow workers.

They had only reached the corner of the house when Sidney hesitated. "The balloon! Look at it! Something is wrong; the tethers have come loose!"

"Isabelle," Henry moaned, setting off at a run.

It was some distance to the field from the house, but they covered the ground in record time. Henry had never felt panic like this before. He could not see her, though he scanned the field. The sense of dread intensified when the basket was dragged over the stone wall boundary into the farmland beyond, the half-inflated balloon having caught the wind and moving at a rapid speed, considering it was pulling a basket behind it and the ropes that had not been released properly.

At the arrival of Henry, Sidney, and the footmen who had followed close on the heels of Henry, Mrs. Daniels started to move out of their reach, screaming Peter's name. He had been following the progress of the balloon, making sure Isabelle did not get out and ready to react if she did. Turning at the sound of panic in her voice, he held out the knife to defend himself.

"I will use it," he snarled but was taken aback when Henry, who was in the lead, ran straight past him without a glance in his direction.

Allowing himself to be distracted by Henry was Peter's downfall. Sidney planted him a facer almost before he comprehended that Sidney had reached him. Peter fell to the ground, holding his jaw, and the knife flew from his hand.

Kicking the knife out of Peter's reach, Sidney towered over the man who had been his friend but had betrayed him in the worst possible way. "Give me one excuse, and I will not hesitate to kill you."

Mrs. Daniels seemed stunned at the events that were happening around her. She'd pulled out her gun when she saw Henry, but like Peter, was distracted when he ran right by her. By the time she realized what was happening, the lead footman had knocked the gun out of her hand and was holding her tight. She started to struggle, pleading her innocence, exclaiming that Peter had forced her into the situation and threatened her that if she did not do as he wished, he would tell her husband that they were having an affair. She only stopped screaming when she seemed to realize that she was drawing attention from the house. And through it all, the footman's grip on her held.

"I am going to hang anyway, so I might as well take you with me, you jumped-up nodcock. It will be worth it to finally put you in your place," Peter snarled, lunging for Sidney.

Several yards away, Henry was still chasing the balloon. He had not responded to anything around him, not even noticing that Peter held a knife. His whole aim was to get to Isabelle, for he knew without doubt that she was in that basket. Never feeling panic and fear like it, he continued to run, fearing the worst but needing to reach her. If he died in the process, at least he would save her. He had to know that she was safe. She had to live… He could not lose her, he just could not.

ISABELLE DID NOT have the luxury of time to think. She instinctively knew that the wicker basket offered her the only protection she would have from being dragged across the ground, so she clung to it for dear life. Her fingers were cut from ramming them between the sharp structure as she tried to grip it, trying to stop herself from being flung about as she was dragged across the field. She was still thrown against the sides as the balloon gained momentum; her body felt battered and bruised, and her fingers screamed with pain, but she could not falter.

Her only reference she had to where she was, was when the top of the basket was visible to her. But as that was mainly angled towards the sky or the trees, she had no idea how far she had been carried along or what obstacles she was going to hit until the balloon came to a rest. Unable to see how inflated the balloon was, she did not know how long she would be able to hold on. If it came to a stop, it would lead to a whole other set of problems, in that she had very little strength left, and her attackers each had a weapon. Feeling helpless, she choked on a sob, thinking she would never see Henry again.

When the basket left the ground, there was some relief from the violent jolting, but as the basket's flights were short-lived, the force with which it hit the ground offset any advantage of being airborne. It would take every ounce of strength for her to keep hold at those moments—the basket thudded down onto the hard ground, knocking the wind out of her.

Isabelle could see the wicker basket was breaking as it was dragged across the landscape. Frantically trying to decide what to do, while battling to not be overwhelmed by the sounds surrounding her, she let out a scream when something made a hole in the side of the basket close to her. If it had torn the wicker she had been clinging on to, she would have been flung out and unable to secure herself, which would be a sure way of being knocked senseless. Without a doubt, if she lost consciousness, she would never wake up again. Peter and Mrs. Daniels would see to that.

At the next lurch, she decided she could not cling passively onto the disintegrating structure any longer; it was becoming more dangerous inside the basket now it was falling apart. It was time to act if she was to stand any chance of getting out alive. She started to move towards the opening of the basket. If she threw herself out of it while she could not see outside, she could end up in a worse situation than she was already. The thought of Mrs. Daniels nursing her until she could find a way of finishing off what they had started was enough to make her falter, but gritting her teeth, she knew she had to do something, or she would end up as broken as the basket.

With the balloon's erratic movements, it felt like it took an inordinate amount of time for her to reach the edge of the basket, which was only at chest height, but she had to crawl, digging her fingers into the wicker before trying to move a little further. While she moved, inch by painful inch, she had come up with only one idea—and the risk to her was almost as great as remaining where she was.

Focusing on the task at hand, she refused to let the fear that threatened to choke her stop her from attempting to save herself. It was clear that if there was one sudden jolt, she could quite easily lose her hold and be crushed by the basket in her fall.

Finally feeling the basket lift off the ground, she scrambled onto the edge of it as much as possible and pushed herself away from the one thing that had, so far, offered her some safety.

Time seemed to stand still as she finally freed herself of the basket. Though she was not too high when she fell, she hit the ground hard and rolled with a grunt of pain. Lying motionless, she struggled to breathe as she closed her eyes in agony.

Chapter Twenty-One

HENRY WAS ALMOST at the balloon when he saw Isabelle appear at the top of the basket. He did not have time to feel any sense of relief that she was alive, for she clearly was unsafe, and as the basket was being flung around, she was very often out of sight.

When the contraption lifted once more off the ground, Henry was gripped by so much terror, he thought his heart might actually stop.

The horror of the moment intensified for Henry when he caught the flash of her dress as she clung to the edge of the basket. Her body seemed to still for a moment and then rise. In some strange way, Henry thought she was in control of the situation before reality hit when he saw her body come crashing to the ground.

Henry did not even register that he was shouting out to her, lungs fit to burst, but he ran even faster while he screamed her name time and again.

Falling to his knees the moment he reached her, he touched her, trying not to move her but needing to know if she breathed. "Isabelle, no! Oh God, no! Please, not her!" he moaned over and over as his fingers moved over her, checking to see any signs of life. Only when he touched her arm did she flinch in pain. "You are alive! Thank God!"

Opening her eyes, Isabelle was disorientated and confused for a few moments, frowning at Henry as if trying to figure out why he was looming over her. Still struggling to breathe, she forced herself to speak, knowing it was important to reassure him. "I wanted to live," she choked out. "But everything hurts, so I am no longer certain it was the best course of action."

Henry choked out a chuckle, struggling to contain tears of relief. "I am so very glad you are alive; hurting sounds to me like it is a very good sign."

"I always thought you had a cruel streak in you." Isabelle felt her breathing ease from the severe winding she had suffered on impact. It had been terrifying to struggle to take a breath, but as always, Henry's presence had made her panic ease.

"Miss Carrington, Isabelle, I am going to be even more cruel, for I need to hold you. I do not think I will believe you are safe until you are in my arms, but it might hurt you more."

"I think I would not mind," Isabelle replied.

"Good." Henry gently lifted her into his arms, pulling her onto his lap. "I thought I had lost you."

Isabelle sighed at being off the hard ground, and though it hurt to move, she leaned into Henry, not wishing to be anywhere else.

They heard a sudden crash, and both looked in the direction of the balloon, which had become completely entangled in the trees in the next field. Having hit the tree, what was left of the basket was now dangling listlessly just above the ground, battered and torn, gaping holes clearly visible. If she had not jumped...

"I do not think I will ever want to be near a balloon again. It is not such a good way to travel as I once thought," Isabelle whispered.

"That is good to hear. I never want to see you facing such danger again." Henry kissed the top of her head, wanting to say so much but knowing it was not the right time.

Hearing a shout behind him, he saw David and some farm-hands running towards them. Holding Isabelle tighter, he glared at David. "Stay away from her. I will kill you if you try and hurt her."

David held his hands up in defeat. "I wish no harm to anyone. I have not the faintest idea what has gone on."

"Your friend decided it was a good idea to start a romance with Mrs. Daniels and kill her husband. Isa—Miss Carrington approached them about it, and they tried to kill her too."

David had paled at Henry's words. "I knew nothing of this, I assure you. I did not like Daniels, but I would never harm him or anyone else for that matter. Peter was always an argumentative fella, but murder? That is something else."

"It seems he fooled us all about the lengths he would go to in order to get away with it."

"I am truly shocked. I never suspected a thing. A romance with Mrs. Daniels? Why would he do that?"

"I have no idea, and at this moment, I have absolutely no interest in finding out. My concern is for Miss Carrington," Henry replied sharply.

"Of course. I am sorry, it has come as a shock, and I forget myself. Can I help in any way?"

The farmhands were struggling with releasing the balloon. "You can go and ask for the doctor to be sent for. I will bring Miss Carrington to the house."

"Consider it done," David said, immediately turning towards the house.

"Would you let me carry you inside?" Henry asked Isabelle. "I do not wish to hurt you, but you are in no fit state to walk."

"You are not carrying me! I will not be responsible for you injuring your back. I can walk perfectly well."

Henry's lips set in a thin line, but he decided not to argue, for the moment at least. Instead, he helped Isabelle to stand, asking her time and again if anything was hurting, if she felt dizzy, or needed to be carried.

Isabelle eventually held up her hand. "I am fine, to an extent. If you let me lean on your arm and you do not mind the slow progress, I will manage perfectly well."

They walked slowly, Isabelle leaning heavily on Henry and trying not to let her fingers mark his frock coat. They were bloody, and her arm hurt, as did her head, and her ankle made her wince in pain every time she put her foot on the ground, but she was determined that she would reach the house without the embarrassment of Henry struggling to carry her.

Passing the field in which the fateful conversation with Mrs. Daniels had occurred, there was no sign of anyone, which struck them both as strange.

As they made their way to the edge of the field, Henry paused, having reached the end of his patience. "I never took you as someone who was bloody-minded to the point of it being to your own detriment, but I now see that you are."

"That is not a very nice thing to say." Isabelle had little energy or inclination to say anything else; she was hurting all over, and her steps were getting slower as the pain increased.

"What is not very nice is seeing you struggle, and yet you will not ask for help. Your limp is more pronounced; goodness knows what damage you are doing to it with every step you are taking. And if I thought you pale before, you are almost translucent now."

"It does seem a longer distance than I anticipated, but we are nearly there."

"You still refuse to let me carry you, though you have not denied anything I have said."

"You cannot carry me."

"One thing I have learned in my nine and twenty years, Miss Carrington, is that sometimes we do not know what is best for ourselves even though it is right before us." Henry swept Isabelle into his arms and strode towards the house. "The speed you were walking at would have taken us a sennight to reach the house, and I have not so much time to waste when you are suffering."

Isabelle squeaked with shock and was sure she was no longer pale, but flushed to the tips of her toes. Unfortunately, it was because of mortification rather than pleasure.

"Put me down," she eventually ground out.

"No."

"That is not very gentlemanlike of you."

"Perhaps I am sick of behaving just how I should, constantly worrying that I should do as others wish and not what I want."

"If you get injured because of your foolishness, I will have no sympathy for you."

"What? You would not nurse me to health? That seems a little harsh."

"It is most certainly not. If you are silly enough to carry my weight, be it on your own head."

"Do I seem to be struggling to you? Am I gasping for breath? Can I not speak while I am carrying you?"

"Well, no, but..."

"Then stop those windmills in your attic from turning. I will carry you upstairs to your chamber, and I will be no worse for it, apart from questioning my opinion of you and your ability to lean towards nonsensical utterings."

"You know full well why I do not wish to be carried; it is mortifying."

"I know why you think I should not be carrying you, but as those are not reasons I agree with or even acknowledge as anything but the experience making you somewhat scatter-brained, I can ignore your words as irrelevant."

Isabelle huffed but could not argue further. He did not seem to be struggling with her weight, and it had been torture trying to hobble on her foot. Finally accepting defeat, she rested her head against Henry's shoulder and was rewarded with a kiss on the head.

The fact that they had seen no one when crossing the field was explained when they arrived at the door of the house. It was chaos inside.

It seemed that Mrs. Daniels still had loyal servants. At the sight of the pair being brought back in the custody of Sidney and the lead footman, they had decided that escape was better than seeing their mistress hang and were battling on her behalf in order to free her from the footmen. However, Henry's footmen were resolute, and were soon joined by other household staff who managed to subdue the woman and her cronies. Ruth had taken the guests out of the way of getting hurt, but Mr. Carrington was seen shaking Peter and demanding to know what he had done with his granddaughters.

If it had not been so serious, Henry would have laughed at the scene, but bending his mouth to Isabelle, he spoke quietly. "Be prepared, I am going to shout."

Isabelle nodded, hating to see the anguish on her grandfather's face, but knowing now that she had started to relax, she would not have been able to stand on her own. Her body was feeling the full effects of what it had gone through, and whereas normally she would have tried to reach her grandfather to reassure him, she could do nothing but watch and let Henry take control.

"Quiet!" Henry shouted above the melee. "I have an injured woman who needs to see a doctor, and I will punish, severely, anyone who delays me getting her to a chamber. Now get out of my way!"

Chapter Twenty-Two

ONCE THE DOCTOR had examined Isabelle, strapped up her ankle and arm and cleaned and bandaged her fingers, he stood at the foot of the bed, rolling down his sleeves. "You probably do not feel it now, but you have been very lucky. Not many would have come out of such a situation mostly unscathed."

"I know how fortunate I am," Isabelle agreed. "If I had stayed in the basket, there would have been no need of your services."

"I will leave some laudanum in case the pain becomes too much. Then again, you are a healthy young woman, so you might not need it. I am confident you will be hobbling about in a day or two."

"I hope so."

"Try to keep the ankle raised as much as possible. Even when you start to move around, rest it often."

"I will, thank you."

"If anything changes at all, send for me and I will return. I have checked you over carefully and cannot detect any other injuries, but I would take things a little slowly for the next few days."

"I am sure I will be fine once the aches go away. I was thrown about a lot."

"You might feel excessively tired, that is perfectly normal. Let your body rest when it wants to; it will all help you to heal quicker."

"You have been very kind."

Sophia had remained with Isabelle whilst the doctor tended to her and saw him to the door when he had finished, giving Isabelle a chance to look around the room to which she had been brought. It was a different bedchamber than the one she had been staying in with Eliza and Sophia. It was as large, if not bigger, but there was only one wide canopy bed in which she lay. The fire was set, but as the day was warm enough, it had not been lit. Two chests of drawers, a small desk and associated chairs were all that filled the room; it was comfortable and functional.

Sophia came back into the room and hugged her friend.

"What was that for?" Isabelle asked with a laugh and then a groan. Her body was complaining bitterly, even against the slightest movement.

"It was that, or I would have had to box your ears! Why did you not take me with you when you went to seek out Mrs. Daniels?"

"I did not intend to challenge her over the accusations initially. I was looking for Eliza, and it seemed the perfect opportunity when I was there. On reflection, it was not one of my best decisions. What has happened to them?" Isabelle's thoughts flew back to the scene in the field, and her voice stuttered. "Mrs. Daniels had a pistol! Is anyone hurt?"

Ruth soothed her with a hand on her arm. "I understand it was not loaded, and the footman who arrived with Mr. Brook knocked it out of her hand. He held Mrs. Daniels, while Mr. Brook subdued Mr. Boyd."

"Poor Mr. Brook. Is he badly injured?"

"The doctor will probably be seeing him now; you were obviously the more urgent patient. I think Mr. Boyd got some punches in, but that is all."

Isabelle was relieved Sidney had not been badly injured. "I should have gone to his lordship," she said.

"Yes, you should have, but it is done now, and thankfully you will be well. If you can survive a visit from your grandfather, of course."

Isabelle grimaced. "I suppose I had better get it over with. I am surprised you managed to keep Eliza out for so long."

Sophia looked a little uncomfortable.

"What is it?"

"No one knows where Eliza is."

"What? I do not understand."

"When we separated to look for her, which I genuinely thought you were doing and not challenging a potential murderer..." Sophia said drily, "I searched the house. She was nowhere to be found and, throughout all the commotion, has not reappeared."

"Where could she be?"

"Your grandfather was out of his mind with worry, thinking you were both in danger."

"I am sorry I could not reach him when Lord Gosforth carried me in, but at that point, I did not have the strength to stand on my own. You had better let him in."

Isabelle was not surprised that as soon as Sophia opened the chamber door, her grandfather entered the room, clearly having waited in the hallway outside.

"Forgive me?" she said to her grandfather the moment she saw his wan complexion.

"You foolish child," he said, kissing the top of her head. "We could have lost you." He sat beside her, taking her hand in his. "I could not have borne it if anything had happened to you; you know how precious you are to me."

"I truly am sorry," Isabelle reiterated. "I should not have gone off the way I did."

"It is over now. I can be thankful that you are safe and will be well," Mr. Carrington said. "I just wish I knew what Eliza is doing. She did not come with you to the field?"

"No. I have not seen her since last night. Are there no clues as to where she could be?"

Mr. Carrington shook his head but was prevented from needing to reply by a knock on the door and the entrance of Katherine.

"I hope you do not mind me popping in. I will only stay a moment, but I just wanted to see for myself that you are safe," Katherine explained.

"I am a little sore, but other than that I am fine. I am mortified that I managed to create such a fuss." Isabelle played down the extent of her injuries.

"Nonsense," Katherine said. "I think it was very brave of you."

Isabelle smiled. "Foolhardy, more like."

"We have been very worried about you," Katherine said.

"Never more so than when she was carried in. I thought it was too late," Mr. Carrington said.

"I am not surprised. Henry said it was a miracle you are alive," Ruth said. "Now, there can be no leaving for the foreseeable future. You are welcome to stay as long as you wish."

"Oh, no! This was going to be your family time," Isabelle said, mortified. "If you could accommodate us for another night, we can remove to an inn, can't we, Grandfather?"

"Henry would throw me out if I agreed to such a scheme, though I would never do it." Ruth smiled. "You will stay here for at least the next week, if not longer. Mother is staying with us, and we have lots of time to become reacquainted."

"I need to find Eliza. I am becoming increasingly worried about her," Mr. Carrington said. "This is out of character for her."

"Perhaps we could speak about that when you have a moment," Ruth said.

"We can step out now." Mr. Carrington stood, worry in his expression.

"We will leave you be," Ruth said to Isabelle. "If there is anything you require, please do not hesitate to ask."

"Thank you," Isabelle replied as they left. "I wonder what is going on with Eliza. Grandfather is right, this is out of character for her."

"I have a feeling that she is not here," Sophia said gently.

"What can you mean? Where could she have gone?"

"I looked in almost every room in the house. You checked outside. There was no sign of her when Mrs. Daniels and Mr. Boyd were brought in, so I honestly think she must have left."

"Alone?"

"I do not know. I presume so."

Yawning, Isabelle did not notice the look of discomfort on Sophia's face, but instead, she laid back on her pillows. "I feel so tired."

"Why don't you rest for a while. There is nothing you have to concern yourself about, and it would probably do you the world of good to have a sleep."

"I know you said that Mrs. Daniels is in custody, but no matter what happens, would you please stop her from nursing me if the situation should arise?" Isabelle appealed, weary but still terrified at the woman's threat.

"She would not be allowed anywhere near you," Sophia said in surprise.

"It was something she said before they put me in the basket, that if I did not die in the balloon, she would find a way to finish me off as I was recovering."

"Oh, my goodness! I cannot believe how truly evil that woman is!" Sophia exclaimed. "I can promise you that neither she or Mr. Boyd will be allowed anywhere near you."

"Thank you, and I am sorry to have caused all this fuss. Eliza would curse me for it, saying I bring these situations onto myself."

"Do not worry about anything for now," Sophia said. "Just concentrate on getting better. And you can start by going to sleep."

"I think you might be right. Who knew that excitement could be so exhausting," Isabelle said, eyes closing.

ISABELLE AWOKE WITH a start. She had been having the worst of nightmares and knew she had cried out. It was probably her shout that had woken her. Heart racing, feeling sweaty and panicked, she nearly cried out once more when she noticed a figure standing at the side of her bed.

"Shhh," Henry said. "You are safe. There is nothing to be afraid of."

"I thought I was back in the basket," Isabelle said. "What time is it?"

"Sometime after three." Henry was in breeches, shirtsleeves and waistcoat, his frock coat draped over a chair near the fire, which had been lit at some point.

"The last thing I remember, Sophia was here. I did not think I would sleep for so long."

"I said that I would stay with you. Miss Belmont had been with you for some time."

"That is very kind of you." Isabelle was fully aware it was completely inappropriate that they were in her chamber alone. Not thinking clearly enough to understand why her grandfather would have allowed Henry to be with her, she lay quietly, trying to forget the horrible dream. "I am almost afraid to go back to sleep for fear of another nightmare."

"I am not surprised you are experiencing bad dreams. It was a living nightmare to see the basket being dragged along, becoming more and more battered."

"I have never been as frightened in my life, and it was caused through my own stupidity."

"Yes, we will be speaking about the course of action you chose when you are well enough to withstand a severe scolding. All that matters for now is that you get well."

"If I am to face a telling-off, I might have to experience a relapse until everyone forgets what happened."

"As the horrific situation is seared into my memory, you would have to suffer an extended relapse of many years."

A silence descended between them, making Isabelle acutely aware that she was in a bedchamber, alone, with the man she had kissed twice. Swallowing to try and control her heart rate, she pulled the blankets further up to her chin.

"Are you cold? I can build up the fire," Henry offered, immediately alert to her discomfort.

"No, thank you. Please do not think me ungrateful to you for sitting with me, but I am surprised that my family allowed you to remain here."

"Ah, I think it is better to speak about that when you are feeling more the thing."

"I am perfectly well."

"The bandages on your ankle, arm and fingers are just to gain sympathy then?"

Isabelle could not help the roll of her eyes. "I am not addle-brained. The injuries are to my body, not my understanding."

"Anyone who saw what you did would quite rightly question your sanity." Henry was doing all he could to divert her attention, but even with only the light of the fire, he could see her expression. He was wasting his breath, but he was not going to give up easily.

"It is very kind of you to offer to stay with me. Does no one know that you are here?"

"I have the approval of your grandfather, who is a little busy at the moment."

Isabelle tried to sit up, wincing when she put weight on her arm.

Henry moved to persuade her to remain still, settling the pillows behind her head more comfortably. "See, this is exactly why I wanted to hold my tongue and tell you about everything when you are feeling better."

"I am ready to hear anything you have to say, especially when it has to do with my grandfather being worried," Isabelle said, teeth gritted against the pulsing pain in her arm.

"Fine!" Henry said, half-amused, half-exasperated. "Your cousin has eloped."

Chapter Twenty-Three

"**W**HAT?" ISABELLE CRIED, struggling even more to sit up.
"Please be still!" Henry appealed. "I cannot face
the wrath of Miss Belmont if you make yourself worse. I
promised her that I would not upset you."

"She knew something," Isabelle said, eyes narrowing as she
recalled Sophia's expression. "Sophia either knew or suspected it,
and she never said a word. I was too tired to question her about
her reticence."

"I wish you were tired now."

Isabelle glared at Henry, which gained her a rueful smile. "I
think you had better start telling me what has gone on. What on
earth possessed Eliza to elope? More importantly, with whom
and when? What happened to change her plan of securing you?
And how did you find out?"

"Would you like me to remain silent while you ask every
question you can think of, or do I have time to answer the
multitude you have already uttered before you take breath for the
next round?" Laughing when Isabelle growled in frustration, he
held up his hands. "I take it from that you would like me to
answer your questions."

"Yes, please," Isabelle ground out.

"It seems your cousin did not wish to return home unmarried; your grandfather explained how he had said she was to

become companion to your mother."

"I know all that," Isabelle interrupted mulishly.

"Easy, my little firecracker. Remember what trouble you get into when you rush into something."

Uttering a harrumph, Isabelle folded her arms. "You are enjoying this far too much."

"I have decided that the rest of my days will be filled with teasing and tormenting you because it is such a pleasurable pastime."

His words had the effect of flustering Isabelle enough that she remained silent. When he raised an eyebrow at her as if challenging her to question what he meant, she shook her head.

"That discussion can wait for a little while longer," Henry said amiably, thoroughly enjoying himself. "It seems Miss Hodge had a conversation with my sister, who thought it prudent to unsubtly hint that my affections were aimed in a different direction."

"Eliza took the hint?" Isabelle did not dare ask which direction.

"Actually, no," Henry said with a grin. "Ruth then decided that bluntness was in order, but apparently your cousin did not take the news well."

"She does not like anyone going against her when she has made her mind up about something."

"No, but unfortunately for her, I would never have entered into a marriage with her."

Henry had said that before, and Isabelle had known, deep down, that he'd spoken the truth, but her natural insecurities breathed a sigh of relief. "It still does not make sense that she would choose to elope, though."

"Your grandfather overheard your cousin's response to Ruth's words and took her to task for being rude to the hostess."

"Oh dear."

"Precisely. He told her in no uncertain terms that with her attitude, she was to be a companion to your mother because they deserved each other."

Isabelle hid her face in her hands. "Poor Eliza."

"I cannot believe you feel sympathy for her," Henry said. "Anyway, it seems she decided that being married to Mr. Sutcliffe was a far better option than being a companion."

"Mr. Sutcliffe? No!" To say Isabelle was shocked was an understatement. "But he is... she cannot... No! You must be wrong!"

Henry laughed at her reaction. "You must believe me, I am speaking the truth."

"But he is everything she dislikes in a person."

"He seemed perfectly reasonable, if a little too outgoing for my taste, but perhaps she wanted that."

"No, oh, it does not matter."

"Those words lead me to believe that it really does matter. What are your objections to him?"

"I have none, and if he is good to her and she is happy with him, I wish her all the best, I really do. It is just that... oh, damn and blast it! He loves his food, and the poor man will be browbeaten over what he eats with Eliza as his wife. She cannot stand gluttony and is very vociferous on the subject."

Henry became serious. "Then I feel sorry for him, but perhaps she has seen that he is a good man and will dote on her."

"I really hope you are correct."

"So do I."

"How has Grandfather taken it?"

"He was shocked, very shocked, as the letter was left by Mr. Sutcliffe and not your cousin. He managed to arrange a special licence, and they will have been married this morning. He instructed that their things should be forwarded on and said they will be going on a wedding trip of a few weeks," Henry explained. "The letter was discovered just after we had returned to the house."

"Poor Grandfather," Isabelle said.

"It is a good match for her, and I think he was coming to

accept that by the time he went to bed."

"I hope she is happy."

"After how she was with you, that is a very magnanimous thought."

"There is no point repining over what has gone on. She had some justification in her dislike when she explained why she felt the way she did. I can only be sorry that she could not have the large wedding I am sure she would have wished for."

"I think having Mr. Sutcliffe's wealth at her disposal will appease her. She has managed to increase her ranking in society and secured her future. She has done well for herself."

"I hope she loves him for both their sakes," Isabelle said quietly.

"And that is why you are a delight. You are such a good person."

"I have many faults."

"I am going to enjoy discovering them, though I hope that putting yourself in dangerous situations was a one-time occurrence."

Isabelle's glare returned. "You are talking in riddles. I do not understand your meaning."

"I am afraid that I will frighten you off, and you will try to run from this room, but whichever sanctuary you seek out, I will follow. It is one of the advantages of owning the house."

"Are you feeling quite the thing?" Isabelle was confused. He was hinting at them having a future together, but she could not be sure that was what he meant. Her head was beginning to pound, and she just wanted him to speak plainly.

"I have never been happier."

"Something is havey-cavey about you, and I insist on knowing what the devil is going on. It is too late for us to be playing games."

"From the first moment I met you, I knew you were something special. Any woman who can curse as well as I was always going to be irresistible."

"If you do not explain yourself in the next two minutes, I am leaving this room and banging on my grandfather's door, telling him that he has left me with a madman."

"You would wake an old man in the middle of the night? I am shocked."

Isabelle let out a curse of annoyance and flung the bedcovers to one side, only pausing when Henry held up his hands in defeat. "You had better start talking, and fast," she warned.

"Fine! I can see 1 will have my work cut out with you. I am going to tell you!" he continued, a laugh in his voice at the glare he was receiving. "I spoke to your grandfather and told him the truth of the matter, of what we have shared, of my hopes and feelings, and thankfully, even with everything that has happened today, he approves and gives his blessing. Still, I really do think we should discuss this when you are feeling better."

"Why would you speak to Grandfather? Why did you reveal everything to him? I think you are one of the most frustrating people I have ever met."

"But I am a good kisser, you must acknowledge that. I do so love it when I make you blush, it is very endearing."

"It is a sign that I am about to explode," Isabelle growled.

Henry moved from his chair and sat on the edge of the bed. "Promise me you will listen to my reasons before you shout at me. I told him we were engaged."

"You—he—you told him what?" Isabelle choked out.

"That we are engaged, unofficially, of course. We were just waiting for the right moment to announce it." Henry was smiling, but there was an air of uncertainty he could not hide.

"And he believed you?"

"Yes. I am not such a bad catch."

"I was not doubting that he would approve of you. I was wondering at him thinking you would be happy with me."

"Oh, we are not going to go over all that nonsense you are very quick to spout every time someone tries to compliment you."

"It is the truth."

"No, it is not. It is the malicious words of people who are not worth bothering with."

"Including my mother?"

"Most certainly. My father was a cruel ogre, and without having met her, I know your mother is cut from the same cloth."

"What did Grandfather say? The truth, please. Every word."

"He shook my hand and wished us both a happy future."

"Really?"

"Of course, he did. Would you expect him to have said anything other than that?"

"I would think he would have been taken aback."

"Apparently, we have been making doe eyes at each other since we met. Everyone has been waiting for something to happen between us."

"I have not been making doe eyes at you! I would not know how to!"

"Oh, but I have?"

"Well, I did catch you watching me a time or two," Isabelle said with a mischievous smile.

"You must have been watching me to have seen me looking at you."

"It was as I was looking in your general direction, not directly at you," Isabelle said airily, trying to stop her giggle.

"It is acceptable for me to be a besotted fool, but not you. I am wounded."

"You are ridiculous."

"But in love."

"Stop." Isabelle held up her hand, all smiles gone. "Please do not say such things."

"It is the truth." Henry had stopped funning and was as serious as Isabelle.

"How can it be?"

"We have kissed. Surely you do not think so little of me that I would kiss just anyone."

"I can believe it was a heat of the moment impulse."

"Twice?" Henry exclaimed. "You could have demanded I marry you after the first time. I most certainly would not have put myself in that situation a second time if I was dallying with you or if it had indeed been just an impulse."

Wiping her hand across her brow, Isabelle sighed. "You say all the right things, but I know what I am, and you could do so much better."

"I am offended on both our behalves for that comment. I can do no more than offer to spend the rest of our lives convincing you that I am worth the risk."

"Of course, you are!" Isabelle snapped. "Anyone with half a brain would be delighted that you wished to marry them. I never thought I would marry, and then I met you, and I longed for a future that had always seemed out of reach."

"Is that a yes?"

"How could I say yes and then be unable to stand to see the revulsion on your face, which I see every time my mother looks at me. I can push aside her distaste to some extent, but it would devastate me to know you felt the same way."

"I would never do that to you." Henry took hold of her shaking hands. "I know you have been treated poorly and unfairly, but there are people out there who value you for who you are. I hope you can trust me enough to be one of those who will treasure you and not want you to change in the slightest."

"I want to believe you. I really do." Isabelle was more torn than she had ever been in her life. She longed to throw herself into his arms and beg him to marry her, and yet she was terrified to take that leap of faith.

"I suppose that is a start." Henry smiled at her. "I do know why you have doubts, and I am willing to say this once, and then I will never mention your body again, apart from to say how beautiful you are."

"But..."

"No. It is my turn now, and I have never been more serious

in my life. I love your body, Isabelle. I loved feeling it pressed against me when we kissed. I loved how it responded to me. I can honestly say that I love your shape because it is a part of who you are, and I love you."

"How are you able to make me feel normal?" Isabelle whispered.

"I am surprised that I can. To me, you are not something so ordinary. You are one of the nicest, cleverest, bravest women I know. That you might have a death wish, well, we can work on that small fault."

Isabelle laughed and squeezed his hands, which were still holding hers. "Thank you."

"Does this mean you will forgive me for telling your grandfather that we are going to marry before actually asking you? I can make a grand gesture if you would like me to."

"I am not one for bringing attention to myself if I can help it. I am happy to say yes now as long as you seal it with a kiss."

"Oh, my sweet girl."

Chapter Twenty-Four

H ENRY SMILED IN delight at Isabelle's request and crawled on the bed until he was above her. He loved that she looked welcoming yet a little unsure. His heart could burst to know that he would be the one to show her the best of what two people could share.

"Let me make one thing clear before I kiss you for a long, long time. I will accept that our engagement does not need any more ceremony than a notice in the *Times*, but when we are married, I want everyone to know that I am the lucky one to have secured *you*."

Isabelle opened her mouth to argue, but Henry leaned forward before she could utter a word and kissed her.

She could not help but respond to him, wrapping her uninjured arm around his neck and pulling him towards her. Smiling when he moaned in approval at her unsaid demand, she arched into him.

Henry rested on one side of her, careful to avoid touching her injured arm and foot. As he continued to kiss her, he very much appreciated that there was only her nightdress between them. He let his hands roam up and down her body, loving the way she moaned in response to his touch.

Pulling away slightly, he smiled down at her. "How fast do you think a large wedding could be arranged?"

"Two months?" Isabelle tried to think coherently, but her body was experiencing too many pleasurable feelings for her to be able to focus properly.

Henry groaned. "Too long. If my mother, Ruth and you all work on it, can it be arranged sooner?"

"You are not offering your own services then?"

"I would only get in the way."

"Why the hurry?"

"Because, my sweet love, I do not think I can wait for months when, selfishly, I cannot wait to experience every part of your gorgeous body."

"Oh."

"Forgive me, I have shocked you."

"A little." Isabelle smiled. "But I also think it would be a shame to wait."

Henry chuckled. "I really do love you, and I hope you never stop surprising me, but I will not force you into a situation you feel obliged to agree to because of my impatience. I will wait."

Isabelle stroked the side of his face with her knuckles. She would have loved to use her fingertips, but as they were all bandaged, she would not be able to feel his skin, and she needed to touch him. She returned Henry's tender smile.

"I want you too, and I hope the fire has died down enough that you cannot see me blush."

Chuckling, Henry kissed her. "Not quite, but I love it, and it makes my heart pound to know you feel as I do."

"I can hardly explain how I feel. All I know is that my insides are aching, but I do not know for what."

"Oh, my love," Henry groaned.

"Please make love to me," Isabelle whispered.

"I would be taking advantage of you. I can give you pleasure without taking your innocence."

"But you would not be satisfied."

"It does not matter."

"It does to me."

Henry groaned even more earnestly. "I can only be a gentleman to a point, and I am rapidly reaching that point. I had better leave."

Making a decision that would have her ruined if something changed and they did not marry, Isabelle took a steadying breath. "I have always behaved as society expects, faded into the background, and tried not to offend anyone by drawing attention to myself. People still condemned me, making presumptions without getting to know me."

"I hate that you have been treated so poorly and not been valued as you should be."

Isabelle smiled. "I am still struggling to accept what you think of me, but I promise to try and believe you."

"Good."

"Part of that belief is going to be me starting to live my life to the benefit of us both, to ignore what has gone on in the past. To trust in you."

"That sounds perfect."

"In that case, would you please stay with me tonight?"

"I will stay but we will wait until your body heals before I make love to you," Henry said.

"Every time you touch me, I forget the pain."

"That makes my heart sing, but I still do not want to hurt you."

"You would not. I long to belong to you in every way. I know you will be gentle and I promise that the pain is not too bad."

"Are you sure?"

She put her arm around his neck to draw him closer. "As sure as I have ever been about anything."

"Oh, Isabelle, I promise you I will spend my whole life making you happy."

"I love you, and I am already the happiest I have ever been."

"Oh, my love, this is nothing," Henry whispered, kissing her deeply. Her words had made his heart melt, and it was even more hers than it had been that first day, when he had seen her stand up to Mr. Daniels. She had been damaged, in some ways, just as he had, and he would spend their future erasing that past.

As he moved her nightdress up and felt the smoothness of her skin over her wonderful curves, he knew without doubt that no one else would ever compare to her.

RUTH FALTERED AT the doorway to Isabelle's chamber. "Oh, I am so sorry!"

Henry blinked himself awake. His eyes stung from lack of sleep, and he struggled to focus. "Ruth, your timing is appalling." His voice was gravelly, his throat dry.

Isabelle squeaked at his words and pulled the covers over her head, making Henry and Ruth laugh despite their own embarrassment.

"I think it is a little late for shyness," Henry said, pulling the blanket away and kissing her head.

"I take it I am to wish you both happy?" Ruth asked dryly.

"Of course. What kind of cad do you take me for?"

Ruth smiled. "I was just checking."

"What must you think of me?" Isabelle moaned, still trying to hide her face.

"Do not worry about me. My firstborn was not really early; it was fortunate we were married a month after, ahem, getting to know each other better."

Henry groaned. "Some things a brother does not need to know."

"I expect you will welcome my help with arranging a quick marriage?"

"Yes, thank you."

"Ah, there you are, brother. I should have guessed," Sidney said, pushing past Ruth and stepping into the chamber.

"Oh, Lord! Are all of your family going to join us?" Isabelle groaned.

Sidney grinned. "Mother is having her breakfast, but I could send for her."

"Stop teasing her," Henry scolded, but his smile was wide. "What did you want me for, you coxcomb?"

Sidney sobered. "That is not as pleasant a situation as seeing you two coming to your senses and making a match of it. It seems Mrs. Daniels and Peter are more slippery than we gave them credit for. They have managed to escape overnight."

"Blast it! Were they being held together?"

"Yes, in the cellar. The footman who was guarding them was attacked at some point. He is being tended to by the doctor as he took a blow to the head."

"We need to send word to Bow Street to try and track them down," Henry said.

"Already done. I sent an express half an hour ago."

That Henry was surprised at Sidney taking control, he did not let show but scowled at his brother. "Then why are you disturbing me?"

"No reason other than to let you know what was happening under your roof. Oh, good morning, Miss Belmont. Welcome to the gathering."

Sophia looked into the room, eyes widening when Henry groaned and covered his head with the covers, too.

Ruth stopped herself from laughing but grinned at Sophia. "We have a wedding to arrange, Miss Belmont. Would you be willing to help?"

"Oh, most certainly," Sophia answered. "Should we gather somewhere we will not be causing any further interruptions?"

"I think that would be best. I will take the liberty of informing everyone to leave Miss Carrington's chamber alone."

"Good," Henry's muffled voice said. "But send food."

Sidney laughed. "We will."

The three left the room, closing the door behind them, their excited chatter echoing down the hallway as they moved away.

"Do you think they have all gone?" Isabelle asked, still hiding.

"I hope so. I think you should check."

"Me? Why me? They are your family."

"And soon to be yours. Besides, it is your friend who saw us."

Isabelle harrumphed and peeped over the top of the cover. "We are alone." She smiled when Henry poked his head out. His face was flushed, his hair sticking out in all directions, and he had never looked as carefree or adorable.

"Let us hope they leave us alone for a month, and the next time we have to leave this room is to get married."

"You would never be so outrageous."

"Is that a challenge?" Henry asked, pulling her on top of him, careful not to hurt her arm or leg.

Isabelle looked as if she was considering his question. Then she kissed him. "I think it might well be."

Epilogue

UNFORTUNATELY, HENRY AND Isabelle did have to leave the chamber before the month was done. Henry complained bitterly about it, but it was an unacknowledged fact that they spent their nights together. The wedding was arranged within a few weeks, to the delight of everyone around them.

Isabelle's mother decided that she quite liked her daughter after all. Though she received a cool welcome from Henry when she visited the family after the announcement of the engagement and would never be a preferred guest, she was happy to go about town gloating that her daughter had secured an earl when the diamonds of the season were still unwed.

The people who mattered to Henry and Isabelle rejoiced that they had met their perfect match. Isabelle sometimes became insecure about her size, but Henry would always kiss her fears away.

When Henry was told that Isabelle was increasing, his own doubts around fatherhood fully came to the fore. That was until he was handed his red-faced, crying son. In that moment, he was overwhelmed with emotion and knew he would lay down his life for his boy and would spend every day of his life making sure his child felt loved and valued.

Eliza had married Mr. Sutcliffe to avoid being left on the shelf. She had never been as furious as she was when Ruth told her that Henry was intent on marrying Isabelle. She had vented her feelings about Isabelle in a way that did her no favours and caused her grandfather to assure her that he was sponsoring her no more; she was to be a companion. Eliza could see no other alternative than to seek out a man she could barely tolerate but had been pleasant to her, force a kiss on him and then insist she had been compromised.

They had no children, and Isabelle was genuinely saddened that the marriage did not seem to be a happy one. Unlike Isabelle's mother, Eliza was not happy for her cousin and though she was relatively pleasant if their paths ever crossed in London, she was loath to utter a good word about them behind their back. This worsened as the years passed and Isabelle and Henry had more children.

Mr. Sutcliffe always looked resigned when with his wife, but he refused to lose any weight however much she insisted. Carving a life spent mainly in his clubs, he was at home very little, which suited them both.

As for Mrs. Daniels and Peter, they disappeared without trace. There was the possibility that they had boarded a ship to the Americas, but Henry promised a large reward if they were ever to land back on English soil. He would not allow them to roam free in the same country as Isabelle. He would always have someone working on the case to make sure Isabelle was safe. That she had no idea of his precautions was a good thing, for Henry knew she would object, but if it meant that he could rest easy, knowing that there was always someone nearby to protect his wife and children if he could not be there, he would stand by whatever expense and subterfuge it took.

Sidney joined the cavalry and excelled in his role, soon being promoted. He was well-liked by his men, seeming to settle into himself now he was secure in his birthright. It would be a long time before he settled down with a wife, but when he did, it was to someone who could love him for who he was and embrace his adventurous nature, though he never went near a hot air balloon again.

Ruth went on to have more boys. She repined that she was surrounded by men, but her mother went to live with her. Though there was a restored bond between Henry and Sidney, Ruth, in particular, welcomed her mother's help and advice after so many years of longing for it.

Isabelle was to have a mother-in-law who appreciated her and offered support in a way her own mother never would.

On the rare occasions Lord and Lady Gosforth went to town, it was commented on how besotted they were as a couple. Some might hint that Lady Gosforth was fortunate indeed to have secured such a handsome man, but anyone spending more than five minutes in Lord Gosforth's company would come away saying: *There goes a man entirely captivated by his wife. There's absolutely no doubt about it.*

And it was completely true.

The End

About the Author

Audrey lives in the North West of England (a Lancashire Lass) and is of the opinion that she was born about two hundred years too late, especially when dealing with technology! She is a best-selling author of Historical Romance, especially the Regency period.

In the real world she has always longed to write, writing a full manuscript when she was fourteen years old. Work, marriage and children got in the way as they do and it was only when an event at work landed her in hospital that she decided to take stock. One Voluntary Redundancy later, she found that the words and characters came to the forefront and the writing began in earnest.

So, although at home more these days, the housework is still neglected and meals are still late on the table, but she has an understanding family, who usually shake their heads at her and sigh. That is a sign of understanding, isn't it?

Find out more at:

www.audreyharrison.co.uk

or

facebook.com/AudreyHarrisonAuthor

or

Audrey Harrison (@audrey.harrisonauthor) • Instagram photos and videos

Milton Keynes UK
Ingram Content Group UK Ltd.
UKHW010826020224
437154UK00013B/499